HEIRS OF Rebellion

VANESSA
MILLER

HEIRS OF Rebellion

MORRISON
FAMILY SECRETS

WHITAKER
HOUSE

Publisher's Note:
Both novellas in this collection are works of fiction. References to real events, organizations, or places are used in a fictional context. Any resemblances to actual persons, living or dead, are entirely coincidental.

All Scripture quotations are taken from the King James Version of the Holy Bible.

Heirs of Rebellion
Morrison Family Secrets ~ Book One

A Two-in-One Collection of Novellas Featuring:
The Blessed One (© 2011 [eBook] by Vanessa Miller)
The Wild One (© 2011 [eBook] by Vanessa Miller)

Vanessa Miller
www.vanessamiller.com

ISBN: 978-1-60374-948-0
Printed in the United States of America

Whitaker House
1030 Hunt Valley Circle
New Kensington, PA 15068
www.whitakerhouse.com

Library of Congress Cataloging-in-Publication Data

Miller, Vanessa.
Heirs of Rebellion / by Vanessa Miller.
pages cm. — (Morrison Family Secrets ; Book One)
Summary: "Christian, family, and romantic themes prevail in this collection of two contemporary novellas, *The Blessed One* and *The Wild One*"—Provided by publisher.
ISBN 978-1-60374-948-0 (alk. paper)
I. Miller, Vanessa. Blessed one. II. Miller, Vanessa. Wild one. III. Title.
PS3613.I5623H45 2013
813'.6—dc23

2013025745

1 2 3 4 5 6 7 8 9 10 11 20 19 18 17 16 15 14 13

The Blessed One

Prologue

Joel Morrison was getting that same gut-wrenching feeling he had back in 1952 when his wife and three children died in a fire. He had been away on location, filming another blockbuster family-friendly movie, when the Kern County earthquake had devastated parts of Southern California, causing widespread power outages in the Los Angeles area. His wife and children had lit candles so they could see, and they must have forgotten to extinguish them when they'd gone to bed. To this day, Joel refuses to allow anyone to bring a candle into his home.

Seven years later, Joel married a sweet-natured woman named Beth. Five children and forty-two happy years of marriage later, she had gone home to be with the Lord.

Joel's children were all grown now and had contributed a lot to the full head of gray hair he'd acquired in his eighty-three years on earth. But not since 1952 had Joel felt like destruction was darkening his door.

He walked into his prayer room with a heavy heart. His knees ached so bad that he no longer bowed down on the ground. These days, Joel either reclined in the comfortable La-Z-Boy chair in the middle of the room or perched on the wooden bench before the altar he'd constructed by hand when he and Beth had moved in twenty years ago. This was the only room in the house that he had kept untouched by the professional decorator Betty had hired. Joel wanted this room to be personal. Pictures of his wife and children hung on the walls. Sometimes he would touch the picture of the son or daughter he was praying for. Joel didn't need much in this room, just his La-Z-Boy, the bench, the altar, and the pictures of his family.

Wanting to be close to the altar, Joel sat on the bench. He looked toward heaven and thanked God for all that He had done for him. In truth, Joel was a wealthy man—a millionaire six hundred times over. And he owed everything he had to the Lord. So, each morning, he rose early, came into his prayer room, and thanked God for life, health, and strength. He also sent up prayers for his children. They were all successful in their own right, and Joel knew that the Lord had made that possible. But God must have been allowing his children free choice with their personal lives, because they were headed in the wrong direction.

"Father, You know more about what's going on with my children than I, but I have this feeling in my gut, and it's telling me that trouble is on the way." Worry lines etched Joel's face as he continued. "I wasn't around to save my first wife and children when they died senselessly. But, Lord, please let me live long enough to see my children trusting in You." He sat there on the bench, waiting patiently for the Lord to show him what to do.

A thought struck Joel. He stood and paced the perimeter of his prayer room. Yes, he had been praying for his children since they were born. He'd read to them from the Bible, telling them many of the great stories within those sixty-six books: Joshua fighting the battle of Jericho, Daniel in the lions' den, and Jonah in the belly of a whale. But he had obviously failed to teach his children the importance of living for God and trusting Him at all times.

"Well, I'm not dead yet," Joel proclaimed. He opened the door and walked out of his prayer room with an idea forming in his head.

It was now years after hurricanes Katrina, Gustav, and Ike, but people were still homeless and jobless. The national unemployment rate was the highest it had been in years; banks and businesses were closing in record numbers. Joel knew of many people who were in need due to the recent economic downturn. And he wanted to help them.

He went into his office, sat down at his massive oak desk, and pulled out his personalized stationery. He was ready for a vacation, and he was going to invite his children to join him. He wasn't sure if they would enjoy this vacation once he disclosed part of his plan. In fact, he knew they wouldn't be happy. But if his plan worked, then before all this was over, his children would renew their relationship with the Lord.

Joel wanted to shout "Hallelujah!" and do a praise dance to the Lord, but he had five letters to write.

One

Mr. Morrison, I really need to discuss something with you before you leave today."

Eric's assistant, Karen, had come into his office just as he was leaning over his desk, putting some files in his briefcase, so he could head home. He straightened up, revealing his full six-foot-two, 178-pound physique. He straightened his buttercream-colored tie and looked at his watch. It was 7:30 PM. He'd promised Linda that he would be home by six. Well, he'd already broken that promise, so he might as well handle this business. He sat back down. "What can I do for you, Karen?"

"I would just like to state for the record," Karen began as she handed him a stack of bills, "I had no clue that this much money was being spent since you put Mark in charge of marketing for your campaign."

It was the Corporate America motto: "Cover yourself and blame the other guy." In truth, Karen's responsibilities included reviewing the finances of his campaign and letting him know if his contributions were insufficient to cover his spending. He flipped through the bills, and then, with a frustrated sigh, laid the stack on his desk. "Why are all these bills past due?"

Karen plopped down in the chair in front of his desk and let out a long sigh. "We haven't received as much in contributions as I originally projected. The election is nine months away, and with nothing significant happening, we haven't given the donors a reason to part with their money."

Here he was, mayor of Cincinnati, fully intending to make the White House his home within the next decade, and he didn't even have enough money to run for Governor of Ohio? What did that say about his chances at the presidency? Was he dead in the water before his presidential campaign even marinated in the delegates' minds? Eric refused to believe that. His father had always told him that God was looking out for him and wanted to see him prosper.

Being the eldest child, Eric had always been called upon to solve problems, starting with his own siblings. If he heard someone say, "Give it back; I had it first," Eric would suggest something along the lines of, "Why don't you play with the truck first, Isaiah, and then, in a little while, you can let Shawn see it, okay?" or, "Look, Dee Dee, there's a prettier doll on your bed. Why don't you let Elaine have this old doll, so you can play with the prettier one?"

Problem solving was in his genes. So, before his pity party got started, Eric decided to search for a solution. He grabbed his calculator and began adding up his debts. He turned to Karen. "It looks like we owe almost five million for various items, including my radio and television ads. How much money do we have right now?"

Karen glanced at the spreadsheet in her hand. "We have about two million in liquid assets."

His father could cover these bills without even blinking an eye. But Eric hadn't asked his father for anything since he'd graduated from college. Sure, he gladly accepted the $50,000 his father sent through his accountant to each of his children every year. His father had also bought him and his siblings their first homes. Everyone but Elaine, that is; she was still too busy saving the world to plant roots anywhere. But Eric hadn't asked his father for anything else since he'd bought the house for Linda and him. When their daughter was born, Eric sold that house and used the proceeds to buy the 6,000-square-foot home they now shared. He wanted to be his own man and make his father proud of his accomplishments. The last thing Eric wanted to do as he neared forty was to beg his father for money. Besides, his father knew that it took money to run for public office; and if he wasn't offering, Eric wasn't asking.

"Okay, then," Eric finally said. "Call all of our creditors and offer them a third of what we owe, and then tell them we will pay the rest over the next three months." Eric had no clue where the money would come from to pay the remaining balances. But in the political arena, you never knew—a scandal could develop surrounding his opponent, prompting more voters to want to oust the incumbent and perhaps even pledge money to Eric's campaign. He hoped he wouldn't have to hire investigators to dig up dirt on Governor McDaniel, but he wasn't opposed to it if the need arose.

He finished his meeting and left the office. Linda was going to kill him. This was the third night this week that he'd arrived home after eight o'clock. She didn't understand how much public service meant to him, how much joy he received from setting policies in place that would help communities for generations to come. Being in public service allowed him to use the peacemaking finesse and problem-solving skills he'd developed as a child. But Linda was always complaining that he was more dedicated to the City of Cincinnati than to his own family.

Eric didn't understand his wife. She had everything a woman could want, and yet she was still unhappy. He had bought her a nice home, and she had a hefty clothing allowance. Yes, he was often late, but at least he came home to his wife every night. Not every woman could say that. But Eric Morrison, the next governor of the great state of Ohio, didn't cheat on his wife. Mention the name Bill Clinton to any politician—enough said. No, sir. Eric wasn't trying to build a legacy just to have it torn down by infidelity. His father had taught him that. Joel Morrison used to tell his sons every chance he got: *A man's name is only as good as his wife says it is.*

Eric had met Linda after college, while he was serving as a lieutenant in the United States Air Force. Linda's father was a colonel in the army, so she'd grown up as an army brat.

Now she's just a brat, Eric thought as he pulled into the driveway. She was never satisfied, no matter what he did for her. And if she didn't get her way, she fell apart.

He walked into the house, took off his hat and coat, and put them in the closet. "I'm home," he yelled.

No one answered back. He looked at his watch and walked out of the foyer in search of his wife. He found her asleep in the living room, stretched out on their beige sofa with a half-empty bottle of scotch by her side. Eric rolled his eyes and turned to walk away. Then he noticed a letter typed on his father's stationery, sitting on the coffee table. He crossed the room and sat down on the edge of the couch next to his wife, catching a whiff of her alcohol-laden breath as she snored.

Shaking his head, he picked up the letter and read.

Son,

I hope all is going well for you and your family. It has been way too long since I broke bread with you and your lovely wife. Just thinking about how much I miss my grandchildren brings tears to my eyes. So, I've decided to invite you all to our vacation home in the Bahamas for a week of fun and family.

I know you'll need time to get things in order at your office, so I've scheduled the vacation for the end of the month. How about it? Can you bring your family to the Bahamas on March 25? I really hope you will be there, because I will be going over some changes to my will.

Love, your father,
Joel

Eric held his breath and leaned back on the sofa. What changes could his father be making to his will? As far back as he could remember, his father had said they would split his fortune five ways when he died. Had something changed?

"What did you say to me?" Dee Dee Morrison-Milner glared across the table at her Bible-toting husband. Actually, she preferred thinking of him as her soon-to-be ex-husband.

"I said I love you, Dee Dee. Please, let's just go home and talk this over," Drake Milner pleaded, his dark brown eyes filled with liquid sadness.

Dee Dee didn't care. She rolled her eyes and turned to face her lawyer, who was seated on her left. She ran her fingers through her fifteen-hundred-dollar weave. "William, can you please tell Drake how much alimony he will receive from me when this is all over?"

While Dee Dee's attorney flipped through his files, Drake said, "What if I don't want alimony? What if I just want you?"

Drake's attorney, Mark Winters, elbowed him and spoke up. "Actually, my client has given up a great deal for this three-year marriage. Alimony is the least Mrs. Milner can do."

"Don't call me that." Dee Dee scowled. "I am Dee Dee Morrison. I insist that you refer to me in that manner during these proceedings." Actually, her name was Dee Dee Morrison-Wilcox-Johnson-Sooner-Milner, but Dee Dee didn't want to think about all her failed marriages. She'd rather just be Morrison again and start over. The only reason she'd even entered into marital mistake number four was because her father had thought Drake was a great catch. According to Joel Morrison, Mr. Drake Milner was one in a million. Well, her daddy didn't have to live with Drake. He wasn't around when Drake opened his Bible and dared to read it to her. He wasn't dragged to Sunday morning worship service when all he wanted to do was sleep in. Dee Dee had been through all that madness when she'd lived with her father. That's why she'd thought she could handle a clone of Joel Morrison. But she'd had enough.

"What did I do that was so wrong, Dee Dee?" Drake protested. "I didn't cheat on you, didn't abuse you. I honored the vows that I made to you."

Dee Dee turned to William. "Can you please tell him how much I'm willing to give him in alimony?"

William cleared his throat and announced, "Ms. Morrison is willing to give you fifty thousand a year for the next three years."

Mark laughed. "How generous you are, *Mrs. Milner,* but it's going to take much more than Daddy's annual allowance to help my client retain his standard of living."

Glaring across the table at Drake again, Dee Dee said, "Did you tell him all my business?"

"The bottom line is this," Mark began. "My client gave up his career to move to LA and become your houseboy."

"I never told him he couldn't work," Dee Dee insisted.

"Oh, really? Is that why you got him fired from the last two jobs he acquired since moving here?" Mark asked.

Dee Dee harrumphed. "That's a lie. Drake didn't like any of those jobs. He wanted to travel with me. I did him a favor by calling his employers. If anything, he should be thanking me, rather than trying to extort more money." She stood up and extended her manicured index finger in Drake's direction. "You're getting out of my house today. Do you hear me? Your days of freeloading are over." She turned and stormed out of her attorney's office, jumped in her red Ferrari 575M Maranello, and sped off. She had no time to waste. She intended to put Drake out of her ten-million-dollar Bel Air mansion that day. She lived thirty minutes away from her lawyer's office. Nonetheless, in less than twenty minutes, she was punching in the access code to her gated home. She parked her car in front of the house and ran inside.

Dee Dee stood in the foyer for a moment with her back against the door. She detested the stale white walls, the white marble floor, and the circular staircase. It was all too calm and drab for her taste. She still didn't understand why she had purchased this house. Maybe she had been on some kind of calm-and-drab kick the year she'd married Drake, but she was way over it now.

She went upstairs to Drake's room, gathered a handful of his shoes and clothes, then opened his bedroom window and threw the stuff out onto the well-manicured lawn. On her third trip to the window, she saw her assistant, Marcia, coming up the walkway.

As Dee Dee dumped Drake's underclothes on the lawn, Marcia waved some envelopes in the air with no acknowledgment of the garments. "I have your mail."

"Just leave it on the table in the foyer. I'm busy right now."

Marcia pulled one of the envelopes out of the stack. "This one is from your father."

Dee Dee was tempted to continue with her work, but her daddy was a peculiar kind of man. You never knew when he might just add an extra check to one of his letters. And she could use some extra money right now. God only knew how much it was going to cost her to get rid of Drake, since he was telling everyone it was her fault he didn't have a job.

She went downstairs, took the letter from Marcia, and opened it. As she read it, her world fell apart. *Daddy's changing his will?* Was her father disinheriting her because of her four failed marriages? Could the old man really give away her birthright just because she didn't measure up to his high standards? Dee Dee didn't really know if this was bad news for her or not, but she knew one thing for sure. There was no way that she could go to the Bahamas without Drake. Not when her share of six hundred million was at stake.

Two

Isaiah Morrison felt as if he had just been blessed with a great and wondrous gift that he wouldn't be able to claim as his own. He'd have to leave the gift in its pretty wrapping and give it to a better man. Most of his life, he had dreamed of the day he would pastor his own church. He'd loved God and followed His commandments since he was a child. After college, Isaiah had attended seminary, and he'd been working in the ministry in one aspect or another ever since. He had been a part of the Restoration Church of Christ for twelve years, and he'd become an employee of the ministry five years ago as the associate minister over the outreach programs. Isaiah had enjoyed every minute of his assignments, because his work was not just a job but a calling from God.

Pastor Smith stood by the bay window in his handsomely decorated office. His eyes danced across the lawn, down the walkway, and over the cross that stood in the middle of the yard as a reminder of Christ's sacrifice. "I came to this church over thirty years ago," Pastor Smith began. "We had about fifteen faithful members back then. I didn't know anything about building funds or increasing membership." Still looking out his window, he pointed to the small building adjacent to the magnificent edifice they now stood in. "All I knew was that God had given me that small church building, and I was supposed to make disciples of the members within it."

Pastor Smith turned away from the window and sat down behind his desk, facing Isaiah. "We now have three thousand members, a radio program, and an outreach ministry." He let out a long sigh, then added, "As the Bible says, I've fought a good fight, and I have finished my race. Now it's time for some young blood to take over and lead our church to the next level."

Isaiah laughed. "I'd hardly call you 'old blood,' Pastor."

"I'm seventy-nine years old. My best days are behind me, Isaiah. I don't have a problem admitting that."

"My dad is eighty-three, and he still gets around like a man half his age. He still travels for missions at least three times a year."

Pastor Smith shook his head. "Your father and I may go out and do the work of the Lord as it needs to be done, but I guarantee you he has aches and pains in places you haven't even conceived of yet." Pastor Smith waved his hand in the air, as if to dismiss any further argument. "It's time that I leave the work of this ministry in more capable hands than mine. I'd like to just sit in the pew and fill up on the Word. So I'm asking, Son, will you accept my offer and take over as senior pastor of Restoration Church of Christ?"

Isaiah wanted to stand up, shake Pastor's hand, and accept the call that was so obviously from the Lord. But he had a problem. His beautiful wife, Tanya, didn't want to be the first lady of this church—or any church, for that matter.

Tanya was still trying to become the next Tyra Banks. She thought that her big break was going to come any moment. The same big break she'd missed in her teens and twenties was going to overtake her in her thirties. Isaiah hadn't seen much happening with Tanya's modeling career, outside of the occasional print ad or runway job. But he would not step on her dreams. Instead, he'd encouraged her by paying for portfolios and modeling classes. He did whatever she needed him to do. So, he didn't understand why Tanya couldn't stand by him with something he knew the Lord wanted him to do. "I need to speak with my wife before I can give you a definite answer, Sir."

Pastor Smith stood up, walked around his desk, and patted Isaiah on the back. "That's fine, Son. You go home and talk with your wife about this. But this is the Lord's will, Isaiah. I don't see how Tanya can argue with Him."

Isaiah smiled and stood up. "We'll see, Pastor. We'll see."

They walked outside and stood in the parking lot, looking at the backside of the church building.

"It's a glorious thing, isn't it, Isaiah?

"What's glorious, Sir?"

"Serving the Lord, knowing that you are in His will."

Isaiah smiled from deep within his soul as he responded, "Yes, Sir. That is truly a glorious thing."

He walked away from his pastor then, afraid that if he lingered too long, he might cry from the pain of wanting something so badly yet not being sure he could accept it. After all, he was a family man, and he had to consider the feelings of his wife and their daughter. He got behind the wheel of his Lexus with an excited but heavy heart and put the key in the ignition. Just then, his cell phone rang. Isaiah looked at the caller display and saw that it was Tanya. He pressed "talk" and held the phone to his ear. "Hey, Honey. What's going on?"

"We just got a letter from your father," Tanya said, her voice bursting with excitement.

Isaiah wished she would sound that excited when he told her his news, but he knew for a fact that her tone would be very different. "Did you open it?"

"Yes. It was addressed to both of us, so I opened it immediately." She sounded absolutely giddy. "Your father has invited us to the Bahamas for a vacation, and get this—he's going to be discussing some changes to his will. Do you think he might be dying or something?"

What type of question was that? His father wasn't dying. Then Isaiah thought of how Pastor Smith told him that his dad had aches and pains in places that he couldn't even conceive of. It was at that moment that it sunk in—the man who had taught him to love Jesus was *really* eighty-three years old. Isaiah didn't care if his father left him ten trillion dollars. He wanted to beg God for fifty more years with Joel Morrison.

"Isaiah, did you hear me? Do you think your father is ill?"

"No, no. Not at all. My father has been in perfect health for more than forty years. He probably just wants to tell us about some changes that will affect us sometime in the future."

"Oh," Tanya responded with a lot less joy.

"I can't wait to see my father," Isaiah said, trying to return a bit of enthusiasm to the conversation. "When did he schedule the vacation?"

"The end of this month," Tanya responded. "Look, I'll talk to you later. I need to go shopping."

"Wait." Isaiah wanted to tell his wife his good news.

"What is it, Isaiah? I really need to go."

What put her in a bad mood all of a sudden? "Never mind. I can talk to you later."

Twenty-seven-year-old Shawn Morrison was rolling down the streets of New Orleans in his Range Rover, blasting "Stuntin' like My Daddy" by Lil Wayne. Shawn really did feel like his wealthy father. Not only did he have enough bling around his neck and on his fingers to feed a starving family for three to five years; he had just come back from negotiations for his new contract with the New Orleans Saints. Thanks to his new title as the Touchdown King, his new contract wasn't just fat—it was obese. He was officially a big baller and shot caller, no longer in need of his daddy's charity.

He pulled into the Mercedes dealership, *Stuntin' like my daddy, stuntin' like my daddy*. He parked his Range Rover, slid out, and swaggered across the lot. Opening the double doors of the dealership, his bulky, six-foot-three, 260-pound frame filled the entryway. He had his arms outstretched as if the Messiah had just arrived. *All hail the king.*

"Harry," Shawn yelled through the dealership.

The dealer came running right away. "Oh, hello, Mr. Morrison. How are you today?"

"Paid," Shawn said with an arrogant tilt of his head. He stood as if he were posing for a picture. "So, I came to see if you want to get paid also. Is my car in yet?"

Harry smiled. "It came in this morning. We have it in the back, waiting on you. Follow me."

"Why is it in the back?" Shawn asked. "A car like that should be out front, being shown off."

Harry quickly responded, "We didn't want anyone else to see it before you, Mr. Morrison." He opened the back door and led the way outside.

The pure black Mercedes-Benz SLR McLaren with light brown Napa leather interior was parked and waiting for Shawn, just as Harry had said. Shawn walked around the street-legal race car, grinning from ear to ear.

"Now, I know this car goes fast like a race car, but we like to caution our drivers against speeding on highways and local streets," Harry explained. "You're not the only one on the road, after all."

"Don't preach to me, man. I got enough of that growing up with my parents." Shawn opened the car door and sat down in Napa luxury. He pressed the button to start the car, then rolled down the window and threw Harry the keys to his Range Rover. "Drive that home for me."

Harry plastered a smile on his face. "Yes, Mr. Morrison."

Shawn turned on the radio and raised the volume until the music shook the car. He sped out of the lot as if he were an emergency vehicle responding to a 9-1-1 call. He'd driven less than five minutes when he was pulled over by the police.

The burly police officer angrily approached the car. "Do you know how fast you were going?" he yelled in Shawn's face.

Shawn smiled coyly. "I was merely mimicking my speed on the turf, Officer."

The officer studied him for a moment, then broke out in a grin himself. "Shawn Morrison? Is that you?"

"The one and only."

"Boy, do you know you were driving a hundred and sixty miles an hour? You could get arrested for driving like that."

Shawn looked at the police officer's badge. "Now, Officer Carter, who is going to win the game for us on Sunday if I'm in jail?"

"You better be glad that I've got money on the game this Sunday." Officer Carter laughed and then shook his head. "I should put you in lockup just so you won't kill yourself before the game."

Shawn raised his hands in mock surrender. "That won't be necessary. I'll slow it down."

"That's all I wanted to hear," Officer Carter said. "I'll see you on Sunday." With that, he walked back to his police cruiser.

Shawn was feeling good as he pulled away without even so much as a warning. Then his cell phone rang. It was his girl, Lily. He'd given her a key to his house and let her move in with him last week. She was the mother of his children, after all. He pushed "talk." "Hey, Baby. What's up?"

"I knew I couldn't trust you!" Lily shouted. "I never should have moved in with you."

Shawn held the phone away from his ear and studied it for a second before pressing it against his ear again. "What's wrong with you? Why are you trippin'?"

"I just opened your mail, Shawn, and I am not happy at all."

"Girl, don't you know it's a federal offense to open other people's mail?"

"Call the postmaster, Shawn. I don't care. I'm packing my bags and getting out of here."

"Calm down, Lily. What was it that bothered you so much?"

"Oh, don't you know? You get one every other week."

Shawn wanted to close his eyes and disappear, but he was driving about 80 mph. He wouldn't press his luck. "Not another paternity test?" he asked, already knowing the answer.

"You guessed it, smart one. I'm done with you. You can work out visitation so you can see our children, but I never want to see you again."

Shawn continued speeding down the street. He was just a block from home. "Don't leave, Lily. I'll be home in a minute, and we can talk about this." She hung up on him.

As Shawn turned the corner, he thought about the two children he had with Lily—three-year-old Shawn Jr. and sixteen-month-old Joel Isaiah. As far as Shawn was concerned, Lily was the best woman for him. She didn't nag him about his comings and goings; she took care of their children and kept his house in order. She was one of the finest women he'd ever seen. Her deep chocolate skin, big brown eyes, and long legs made him melt every time he saw her. Why he kept cheating on her, he couldn't even explain. Since he'd been involved with Lily, he'd had to take two other paternity tests, both of which had proven that the children were not his. But now, another woman was claiming he'd fathered her child.

He pulled up in front of his house and jumped out of the car. Lily was putting a box in her own car. She turned to go back inside, and Shawn followed her. "What are you doing, Lily? Why are you letting some female come between us?"

In the entryway, she grabbed another box and turned to go back outside.

Shawn took the box out of her hands. "So, you're just going to ignore me?" He blocked the exit. "You're just going to leave me?"

"Get out of my way, Shawn."

He noticed then that neither of his sons was pulling on his leg, as they usually did when he got home. He set the box back down and glanced around. "Where are my boys, Lily? What did you do with them?"

"They're at my mother's. That's where we live now."

"No," Shawn declared. "You and our sons live with me. We are a family."

A tear rolled down Lily's cheek. She shook her head. "You don't want us."

"What do you mean, I don't want you? I moved you into my house. I've stuck by your side. I take care of my kids. How does that say I don't want you?"

"I'm tired, Shawn. This is the third time another woman has claimed that you fathered her child."

"Exactly!" he exclaimed. "And if you remember correctly, I was proven *not* to be the father those other two times. So, what makes you jump to the conclusion that I fathered this new baby?"

Lily pounded her fists in his chest as tears streamed down her face. "You don't get it, do you? You were involved with those women, Shawn. That's why you had to be tested. You cheated on me."

He grabbed her wrists to stop the assault. "I know, and I'm sorry for that."

She snatched her hands away from him. "Tell that to your next woman. I don't care anymore."

"Okay, okay. Where is the letter? Tell me the name of this woman I'm supposed to have impregnated."

Lily glared at him with eyes full of hatred, and then she walked over to the table in the entryway, picked up a stack of mail, and threw it at him. Several envelopes hit him in the face before landing on the floor. When he bent down to pick up the mail, he noticed an envelope from his father, but he couldn't be bothered to open it at the moment. He grabbed the court papers and read the name Mimi St. Anon. The name didn't even ring a bell.

He looked up and saw Lily standing in front of him with her arms crossed, tapping her foot. "Well, who is she?"

He raised his right hand as if he were giving testimony in court. "I swear I don't remember this woman, Lily. Now that's got to mean something."

"Mmph," she murmured. "It means my mother was right. I never should have gotten involved with you." She walked past him, picked up her box, and kept walking right out of his life.

Three

Sealing the envelope of the first Dear John letter Elaine Morrison had ever written brought tears to her eyes. The whole situation felt wrong. Like God was telling a joke, her life was the punch line, and everyone was laughing but her.

Elaine had dedicated her life to serving others. She had traveled the mission field with her father since she was a kid. After graduating from nursing school, she'd gone to Uganda, Africa, to help with the medical needs of the people there. In the wake of Hurricane Katrina, Elaine had traveled back to the States to help with the cleanup efforts. That's how she had met John Myers. He was strong and athletic, with a heart to serve God's people. After her first date with John, Elaine had called her father and told him, "You won't believe this, Dad. I met someone who reminds me of you and Isaiah."

"Is that good or bad?" Joel had joked.

"Oh, Daddy, you know it's good. His name is John Myers, and he is a humanitarian who loves God."

Tears spilled onto the envelope as she remembered her dad saying that he couldn't wait to meet John. She looked at her left hand, at the princess-cut diamond ring she adored. How she wished that fairy tales did come true.

Wiping the tears from her face, even as the waterfall continued, she made up her mind. The ring had to go back. She would mail it all the way from Uganda. John might want to give this lovely stone to the woman he would eventually marry. She slid the ring off her finger, stuffed it inside a padded envelope, and added the smaller envelope containing her Dear John letter. After sealing it, she got in her Jeep and headed to the post office.

She drove without noticing her surroundings. Nothing mattered to her anymore. Not after the news her doctor had just given her. She needed to pray, but she just didn't believe it would make a difference. Elaine had trusted God with her life, but that hadn't kept her world from caving in. No, she couldn't rush into prayer, because she was still trying to figure out how to trust God again.

She pulled up in front of the post office and sat there, her hands tightly gripping the steering wheel, as she watched people walking aimlessly by. They had no clue that life could be peaceful in one moment and chaotic the next. *Hopefully they will never discover just how cruel life can be,* Elaine thought, as she opened her car door.

Inside the post office, she stood in line behind a woman whose three children—two girls and a boy—were running around, knocking over everything in their way. The mother appeared young and frustrated. She gave Elaine an apologetic smile after failing to rein in her children. "They don't normally act like this," she assured her. "My next-door neighbor gave them candy."

"I think they are wonderful," Elaine told the woman. "You should cherish every moment you have with them."

The woman smiled and touched Elaine's shoulder. "Thank you."

When it was Elaine's turn, she purchased stamps for the envelope and tried not to cry as she handed it over to be mailed. Before leaving, she stopped at her post office box to check her mail. A current of emotions washed through her heart at the sight of an envelope embossed with her father's name and address. She leaned against the wall of mailboxes and whispered, "How did you know that I needed you right now, Daddy?" She closed her eyes and wondered if God had somehow orchestrated her father's letter to arrive on the very day she most needed to hear from him.

But then she convinced herself that God had nothing to do with this coincidence, because it certainly didn't seem as if God cared what happened to her.

"Are you sure about this?"

Joel sat in his home office with his friend and attorney, Gary Dobson. "I'm sure, old friend. God's got a blessing in store for my children. I just need to get out of the way, so He can get it to them."

"I don't know, Joel. I think your kids are going to have you committed for even suggesting such a thing." Gary laughed and then added, "Shucks, I'm tempted to have you evaluated myself."

Joel chuckled. "You go ahead and try it. I'm in my right mind. I'm just a man who has trusted God all my life, and I see no reason to stop now."

"If you say so." Gary opened his briefcase and took out the new will Joel had requested. He handed it to Joel. "Take some time to look it over, and if everything is as you wish, drop by my office so you can sign it."

"Okay. I'll take care of it right after my prayer time."

"When do you leave for the Bahamas?" Gary asked.

"Next weekend. I'm going to get there a few days before the kids, so I can make sure that everything is in order. I really want everyone to have a good time. Maybe if they relax enough, they'll be just as excited about my plan as I am."

"You really believe that?"

"Think about it, Gary. My children are successful; they have money, and they all believe that they are going to have a whole lot more when I die. But are they happy? Do they enjoy life? No, their lives are a mess. They think I don't know, but I'm no fool. As much as I've prayed for them, my children still need Jesus."

"Isaiah and Elaine serve the Lord."

"Yes, they do. I'm thankful for that. But something is going on with them, too. I just hope they will open up to me while we're on vacation and tell me what it is."

Gary lifted his water glass. "May God be with you, old friend."

"And may I live to see the day all my children allow God to be with them."

Four

Eric, Isaiah, and Shawn—politician, preacher, and playboy—relaxed on lawn chairs underneath the covered veranda at their father's beachfront house on Paradise Island. Eric and Isaiah's wives had taken the children to the beach. Shawn had traveled alone. His children were still in New Orleans with Lily, his ex-girlfriend. Their dad and Elaine had been the first to arrive at the house. The trip had exhausted them, so they had decided to take a nap before dinner. Dee Dee and Drake had yet to show up.

"So, when do you think the queen will make her royal entrance?" Shawn asked his brothers.

Eric laughed as he slid off his sandals, put his feet up on his lawn chair, and leaned back. "Dee Dee will stroll in at dinnertime, when we're all together in one room, so that each of us can sufficiently admire her together."

"Such a drama queen," Shawn muttered.

Isaiah pulled off his Bahamas T-shirt that screamed "I'm a tourist," exposing his well-chiseled abs. "You guys have Dee Dee all wrong. She was the third-born child out of five. So, I don't think her issues stem from being a drama queen. I think she is dealing with middle-child syndrome."

Eric scoffed. "Did you have to take psychology to get that divinity degree?"

Isaiah shook his head. "I don't need psychology. I just take the time to try and understand people I care about." He turned and jumped into the pool.

As Isaiah did his first lap, Shawn turned to Eric. "Why do you always give him a hard time?"

"I'm not giving him a hard time. He just thinks he knows everything, and I was simply informing him that he doesn't."

"Don't worry, Big Brother. We are all well aware of who the know-it-all of this family is."

Eric smiled and put his hands behind his head. "And don't you forget it, Little Bro. I wasn't valedictorian of both my high school and college because I know only a few things."

"Whatever."

"Don't be jealous. You don't have to be a brainiac, as long as you can throw that sheepskin and run those yards."

Shawn stood up with his fists clenched. "Are you saying I'm stupid?"

Eric held out a hand. "Relax, Little Bro. You had to have at least a 2.0 GPA to stay on the football team, so you're not stupid, just average."

Shawn's eyes blazed with fury at the insult. He turned away from his brother, sat back down on his lawn chair, and folded his arms.

Isaiah got out of the pool and immediately noticed the tension between his brothers. "What's wrong? What happened?" He started drying himself off with one of the pool towels.

Shawn rolled his eyes and continued to pout but said nothing.

Isaiah turned to Eric. "Did you do something to Shawn?"

"Why don't you tell me what I did, since you seem to know so much," Eric said, then got up and marched away from the patio.

Isaiah flung his wet towel at Shawn. "What just happened here?"

Shawn unfolded his arms and sat up. "I don't know what's gotten into him. But if he tries to insinuate that I'm stupid again, I'm going to knock him upside the head."

Isaiah was pensive as he plopped down in the lawn chair next to Shawn. "Well, something is wrong with Eric, I guarantee you that. He's normally the first one to give an encouraging word to all of us."

"Tell me about it," Shawn said. "When I told everyone that I wanted a football career, Eric was the first to assure me that I would make it to the pros. Now he's telling me that I'm no better than average."

"Would you help me pray for Eric?" Isaiah asked. He stretched out his arm, inviting Shawn to join hands with him in prayer.

"Prayer," Shawn spat with a shake of his head. "That's your answer to everything, isn't it?"

"The Bible tells us that men ought always to pray."

Shawn stood up. "I hate to break it to you, Isaiah, but I haven't exactly been on speaking terms with God in years. So, I think you need to pray for me *and* Eric." He turned and walked away.

"I will," Isaiah said quietly, as he dropped his hands in his lap.

Joel sat at the head of the dinner table. It had been three years since he'd vacationed with all of his children. Right before Beth had passed away, they had taken a trip to Italy with the kids. Joel glanced longingly at the chair at the other end of the table. Beth used to sit there. Her seat was empty now, and even surrounded by family and a table full of his favorites—pasta salad, shrimp, lobster, and mixed vegetables—the reality of her absence still pained Joel's heart.

His eldest son, Eric, sat on his right side with his wife, Linda, seated next to him. Isaiah sat on his left side, his wife, Tanya, next to him. Elaine sat next to Tanya, and Shawn sat next to Elaine.

Eric's side of the table was half full, since Dee Dee and Drake still hadn't arrived.

Joel leaned toward Eric. "Do you think the children are okay with eating at the kitchen table?"

"Are you kidding?" Eric smiled. "They're delighted that they don't have to sit with stuffy old adults."

"All right, then," Joel said. "Let's say grace and then eat up."

As the family bowed their heads, the doorbell rang. Mary, the housekeeper, hurried out of the kitchen and into the foyer to open the door, as Joel finished saying grace over the food. The house burst full of energy as Dee Dee walked into the dining room. She slung her white Gucci purse on the chair next to Linda, then walked over to Joel, bent down, and kissed him on the cheek. With pouting lips, she asked, "Do I mean so little to this family that you would start dinner without me, Father?"

Joel patted his daughter's diamond-bedecked hand. "Of course not, dear. But your brothers and sister managed to get here on time, so I didn't want to make them wait any longer for dinner."

"Maybe your other children don't have as busy a life as I have," Dee Dee said.

"Oh, we're pretty busy," Eric told her, "we just respect other people's time."

Dee Dee rolled her eyes heavenward, then straightened and brushed off her yellow and white sundress. "Well, I didn't mean to get here so late, Daddy, but the traffic from the airport was horrible with all the tourists, and Drake drives like an old lady."

"Where is Drake?" Joel glanced around the room.

"He's parking the car," Dee Dee said with a flick of her hand. "I had him drop me at the door."

Elaine glanced under the table. "You sure wouldn't have been able to walk on that rock pathway with those three-inch heels on."

Dee Dee looked at Elaine, and then her eyes panned the rest of her family, as if she were just noticing their presence. "Oh, hello everyone," she said, almost as an afterthought.

The group all responded in kind. Then Dee Dee turned back to Elaine. "My shoes are from Versace on Rodeo. So, no, I wasn't about to walk on that monstrosity of a walkway."

Drake entered the dining room, waved his hand in the air, and yelled, "Hello, good people."

The family responded jubilantly to his greeting. Eric and Isaiah got out of their seats and shook his hand. Shawn hollered, "How ya' be, Brother-in-law?" And Drake leaned down and hugged Elaine and Linda, as if they were some long-lost family members he was excited to see again.

Dee Dee put her hands on her hips. "Why didn't anyone greet me like that?"

"You get what you give, dear Sister," Shawn said as he piled food on his plate.

Isaiah walked back around the table and hugged his sister. "It's good to see you, Dee Dee."

When he released her, Elaine stood and embraced her. "I'm glad to see you, Girl. You're looking very pretty. I've always told you that you and Angela Bassett could be twins."

"Thank you." As Dee Dee backed away from Elaine's embrace, she picked at the lint on her sister's cotton shirt. She turned up her nose and shook her head as she lowered her eyes to Elaine's faded jeans. "You really need to come out to LA so I can take you shopping."

Elaine looked down at her outfit. "It doesn't look very nice, huh? I probably should have put on a dress or something."

"It probably wouldn't have mattered," Dee Dee said as she started for her seat. "Most of the dresses you have are just as bad."

"What Elaine has on is fine," Linda said, breaking the silence she had maintained since sitting down for dinner. "You're just so hateful, you have to find something evil to say."

Dee Dee scoffed as she turned to her sister-in-law. "I wouldn't expect you to know anything about fashion, Linda. You've gained so much weight, I doubt you've been inside a boutique in years."

"Hey!" Linda stood up shakily and walked toward Dee Dee with her index finger extended. "Why do you always have to put us down?"

"What are you talking about?" Dee Dee asked, eyes wild with bewilderment.

Linda tripped over her feet, almost fell, but then righted herself as she walked around the table and came to stand in front of Dee Dee.

"Linda, sit back down," Eric commanded her.

"No, I have something to say to Miss High-and-Mighty," Linda told Eric. Then, indicating the occupants of the table with her index finger, she turned back to Dee Dee and said, "You're constantly putting all of us down. And I'm sick of it."

"It's okay, Linda," Elaine said quickly. "Dee Dee is right. I should go shopping more often."

Linda turned to Elaine and patted her honey-toned face with her hand. "Y-you really need to s-stop being Dee Dee's doormat, Honey."

Dee Dee turned to Joel. "Since when do you stock liquor in this house?"

Eric jumped up and grabbed his wife. He turned to Joel. "Linda is tired, Dad. She hasn't been feeling well. We're going to turn in for the night, so if you could have Mary bring us some dinner, I'd appreciate it."

"Sure, Son. I'll have some food sent right up to you," Joel said, his heart heavy as he watched Eric hustle his wife out of the dining room.

Dee Dee grabbed the chair next to Joel's. "If Eric isn't going to need this seat, I'll sit next to you tonight, Daddy." She sat down and put some mixed vegetables and a lobster on her plate, evidently oblivious to the part she played in the chaos that had just unfolded.

Five

Isaiah held hands with his daughter, Erin, and walked the beach with Shawn, who carried their niece, Kivonna.

"I want to go in there, Daddy," Erin said, pointing at the ocean.

Erin was six years old, but Isaiah didn't like for her to run off or take too many chances. "There's too much motion in the water for you to get in right now. But you and Kivonna can build houses and castles in the sand while we wait for the waves to calm down."

"Is it okay if we play in the sand over there?" Erin pointed to a hilly area that was devoid of any other children.

"Yes, go," Isaiah told her. Shawn set Kivonna down, and the girls took off running.

Isaiah turned to his brother. "So, why didn't you bring the boys with you this weekend?"

Shawn stuffed his hands in the pockets of his long denim shorts and turned toward the waves. "Lily left me."

Isaiah put his hand on Shawn's shoulder. "Didn't I tell you that Lily wouldn't wait forever for you to make up your mind about marrying her?"

Shawn shook his head. "If that was my only problem, I would just set the date and be done with it. But Lily is through with me."

"What makes you so sure?" Isaiah asked.

Shawn turned from the waves to watch Erin and Kivonna play in the sand. "I have to take another paternity test next week. Lily was home when the court papers arrived."

"Shawn, no!"

"Daddy, Daddy! Look at our castle!" Erin screamed from her position on the hill.

Isaiah and Shawn climbed the small hill so they could view Erin and Kivonna's masterpiece. Isaiah's eyes were big with praise as he told the children how much he admired their artistic and architectural skills. The castle was leaning to the left, but he wasn't about to mention that.

"When do you want to move in, Daddy?" Erin asked.

"Silly," Kivonna said. "You can't live in a sand house."

"It's still pretty," Erin said.

"It sure is," Shawn acknowledged.

Isaiah grabbed Shawn's arm and pulled him to the side. "We need to finish our conversation. I don't understand how you could let this happen again."

Shawn held up a hand. "Not now, Isaiah. I'd much rather hear about you being offered the senior pastor position at your church."

"Changing the subject?"

"You know it," Shawn said with a smile.

"I guess Dad told you about the offer?"

Shawn nodded.

Isaiah moved away from the hill so that the kids would be out of earshot. "I didn't want word of this to get out because I'm not sure what I'm going to do about it."

"What are you talking about? This is what you've always wanted."

Isaiah sat down in the sand. He didn't respond to his brother but stared out at the darkening sky, a sure sign of an imminent storm.

Shawn sat down next to him. "Isaiah, when we were kids, you built your own podium. You preached to each of us every chance you got, and you've told me on numerous occasions that you want to pastor your own church. So, what changed?"

"I have a family now," Isaiah explained.

"So?"

"See, that's why you're having problems with Lily. You put everything above family. I don't know if I can do that."

"How would following your heart's desire to become a pastor harm your family?"

Isaiah glanced at his daughter. There was so much love in his heart for that little girl. He'd do anything for her, even give up his heart's desire. So he turned to his brother and told him straight, "Tanya says she'll leave me if I accept this position. She doesn't want to be a preacher's wife, and I can't let her take my little girl away from me."

Shawn stood up and started pacing back and forth in front of Isaiah, kicking around the sand. He finally stopped and looked at him. "But she knew that you were destined to become a preacher."

Isaiah got to his feet. "That's what I thought too, Bro. But, just within the last two years, she has become adamant about not going into ministry with me."

It looked as if steam might blow from Shawn's nostrils. "That's not right." His hands curled into fists as he turned, still mumbling "That's not right," and walked away.

"What are you doing?" Linda screamed as she watched Eric pour the contents of her 2-liter 7-Up bottle down the toilet.

"I knew you sneaked liquor into my father's house, and I wasn't going to rest until I found it," Eric told her with a self-satisfied smirk.

She rushed at him and grabbed the bottle. "Give it here. It's mine."

Eric blocked her with one arm and continued pouring with the other. "You will not disrespect my father's house like this. I won't let you."

"Why can't you leave me alone, Eric? Why can't you just let me be?"

He threw the plastic bottle in the trash and walked out of the bathroom into the adjoining bedroom. "You're my wife, Linda. You knew what you were getting into when I asked you to marry me, and I just don't understand why you are trying to destroy my life."

Linda followed him out of the bathroom. "Destroy your life? You must be kidding. What about what you've done to me?"

"What did I do to you, Linda? I gave you a beautiful home, our children, and respect in our community...all of which you are trying to tear down."

"You and your endless campaigning has destroyed me," she said, her voice rising in anger, "and you have the nerve to stand there and blame me for what has happened to us?"

"Lower your voice," Eric told her with his finger in her face. "You will not continue to humiliate me in front of my family."

At six feet two, Eric towered over Linda, who was only five feet five. But she didn't care. If getting plastered in front of Eric's father was the only thing that would grant her an audience with her husband, she would get drunk every night of the week. "I don't care what your family thinks of me. I'm tired of pretending that I'm this perfect wife."

He grabbed a pair of socks from his dresser drawer and sat down on the bed. "You'd better get used to it, Linda. Perfect wives sell in the political world; drunk wives don't."

"Tell me something, Eric." Linda sat down next to him and put her hand on his shoulder. "How much is enough for you? I'm mean, you're already mayor of a big city, and now you're running for governor."

Eric put on his socks and then turned to his wife. "You just don't get it, do you?"

"Oh, I get it." She stood up again and used her most venomous tone. "Your daddy isn't as impressed as you thought he would be with your little mayor job. So, you spend your nights networking instead of being home with your family, all so you can become president of the United States and finally receive the praise you desire from your father."

"That's not fair, Linda." He stood, walked to the closet, and pulled out a button-down oxford. "I know I'm gone from home a lot. But I'm networking with people who might be able to help me in the years to come."

"Well, we need you at home."

He put his shirt on and buttoned it. Without looking at Linda, he said, "And, just so you know, I don't need to become governor to make my father proud. He's happy that I'm a mayor. I want to be governor, and, yes, president of the United States, because I believe I can make a difference for this country."

Linda folded her arms across her chest. "What is your family supposed to do while you're out saving the world, Eric?"

"Take up a hobby, Linda. Do anything you want, except drink yourself onto the front page of one of those tabloid rags." He put on his shoes and then left the room.

Now Linda was really fuming. Here they are, on a family vacation, and Eric gets dressed and leaves without asking if she wants to hang out with him. She put up with that type of stuff at home all the time, but she was not about to let Eric get away with leaving her alone while they were on vacation. She walked over to the door, pulled it open, and headed for the stairs. At the top of the staircase, she heard footfalls on the back steps and wondered if

Eric was coming back to their bedroom. She stood at the top of the stairs, holding on to the railing.

She wanted to see Eric's face when he came out of the room in search of her. Let him know how it feels to be left alone.

But the person who came up the stairs wasn't Eric. It was Shawn. He knocked on Isaiah and Tanya's bedroom door. Tanya opened the door, and Shawn said to her, "I left Isaiah at the beach. We need to talk."

Then Tanya stepped aside and let Shawn walk into her bedroom.

Six

Joel came into the dining room and found Elaine sitting at the table, using her fork to toss her pasta from one side of the plate to the other.

"How are you feeling today?" he asked her.

"I'm doing better, Dad, thanks," she replied.

Joel sat down across from Elaine. The cook, Mary, came into the room. "Good afternoon, Sir. What would you like to drink?"

"Iced tea, please." He pointed to Elaine's plate. "What's in the pasta that you fixed today?"

"Grilled shrimp and chicken in a light cream sauce, just the way you like it," she replied.

Joel inhaled and rubbed his stomach. "That sounds good." He stood up and grabbed a plate, knife, and fork off the buffet table, then sat back down. The food was already on the table, so he took the lid off the pasta bowl and served himself a portion of pasta.

"I'll get your tea," Mary said, turning back to the kitchen. She paused beside Elaine, who was still playing with her food. "Is something wrong with your pasta?" Mary asked her. "Would you prefer something else?"

Elaine quickly dropped her fork. "Oh no, Mary, I enjoyed the meal. I just get full so quickly these days. I feel bloated, and I just haven't had a big appetite lately."

Mary nodded and left. Joel put his hand over Elaine's. "Honey, are you sure you're getting enough rest? Don't get me wrong, I think the missionary work you're doing in Uganda is wonderful, but I sometimes wonder if you shouldn't take a little time off."

"I can handle it, Dad. Besides, I love my job."

Mary delivered Joel's iced tea and then left the room again.

"Okay, I'll leave you alone," Joel said to Elaine as he twirled his pasta around his fork. "Where are your brothers and sister?"

"Oh, everyone has gone their separate ways. Shopping, swimming, sightseeing."

"So, why are you sitting in here with your old man when you could be out swimming with your brothers?"

"How do you know Dee Dee isn't swimming?"

"Just a hunch. She seems more the shopping type."

Elaine laughed. "They all left pretty early, and I didn't want to leave before I put a call through to Uganda."

"How is Natua doing?"

Natua was the three-year-old orphan Elaine was helping to raise. After Natua's father died of AIDS and her mother died of starvation, the only person she'd had was her grandmother. That is, until the little girl had found a place in Elaine's heart. "Her grandmother says that she is getting into everything that's not higher than her arms can reach." Elaine shook her head. "That child is a handful, and I love her for it."

"Have you talked to John about adopting her?" Joel saw the sadness creep into Elaine's eyes and quickly said, "The only reason I ask is that since you're planning to marry John, he needs to be in agreement about adopting Natua."

Elaine took a deep breath and moved her chair closer. "I need to talk with you about John and some other things."

"What's wrong, Buttercup?" Joel asked.

"Buttercup?" Dee Dee strode into the kitchen, followed by Drake. "I thought we heard the last of that stupid name at

Elaine's eleventh birthday party, when she begged you not to call her that."

Joel stood up and hugged Dee Dee. "Won't you join us?"

Drake shook Joel's hand. "Good afternoon, Sir."

Joel smiled. Of all the sons-in-law Dee Dee had brought home through the years, Drake was his favorite. The young man treated his daughter with kindness, and above all, he loved the Lord. Joel had respect for the man. "Sit right here, Drake." Joel pointed to the chair next to his. "I want to hear all about this new publishing business of yours."

Dee Dee sat next to Elaine and grabbed a banana and an orange out of the fruit basket on the table. She glanced at Elaine's plate and grimaced. "Do you know how many pounds I would gain if I ate something like that?"

"It's actually very good," Elaine told her.

"And she hasn't eaten much of it anyway," Joel added.

Drake grabbed a plate and sat down. "I'll try it."

"That's my boy." Joel patted him on the back. "Fatten up like the rest of us."

"Mmm, this is good," Drake confirmed after he'd taken a bite.

"Now tell me about your new business," Joel reminded Drake.

Drake nodded. "The last time we talked, I told you about my idea to publish Christian books that truly speak to the reader's heart. Well, I have six authors on my line so far, and we are ready to go to press with four books this year."

"Oh, books, smooks. Drake, tell Daddy about the other business opportunity we just discussed," Dee Dee demanded.

Drake looked at his wife, and Joel's heart was warmed by the expression of patience and gentleness on his face. "We haven't come to any conclusions on that yet, Honey."

Dee Dee waved her husband's comment off and turned to Joel. "Drake is just being modest, Daddy. You know how he is." She looked at her sister and rolled her eyes heavenward, then returned her gaze to Joel. "Daddy, you know what a hard time I'm getting from some of these studio heads about the family-friendly films I want to do. So, Drake and I decided to open our own production company."

"That's great, Dee Dee. With you acting in the films and Drake managing the business, I can see nothing but success in your future," Joel said.

Dee Dee rested her elbows on the table and leaned forward. "So, do you think it's a good enough idea to invest in?"

"What's the investment? Maybe Eric and I will want a piece of it," Linda said as she walked into the room, picked up a plate off the buffet table, and sat down with the group.

Later that night, when Linda was alone with Eric, she told him, "You need to talk with your father about donating to your campaign before Dee Dee takes every dime he has for her stupid production company." She strutted back and forth, biting her nails as she pondered the situation.

Eric kicked his shoes off and stretched out on the bed. "This coming from the woman who wants me to stop networking and sit at home. Why would you care if I got all the money I needed for my campaign or not?"

"I'm a realist, Eric. You are a born politician, and nothing I say is going to stop you. So, the least I can do is try to help you get the money you need for this campaign."

He sat up. "Okay, so why do you think Dee Dee's asking Dad for money will prevent him from donating to my campaign?"

"You know your sister, Eric. Her fair share isn't going to be enough. She always has to have more."

"Yeah, but Dad knows how important this campaign is to me. I can't see why he couldn't help Dee Dee and donate to my campaign."

"Are you kidding me? Investing in a movie production could cost your father hundreds of millions." Linda sat down on the bed next to Eric and put her hand on his cheek. "Honey, you haven't even told your father that your campaign is in debt. You haven't even told me, but I know you. I know when something is bothering you. Why can't you just let your pride go and confide in your family?"

Eric stood up and walked over to the window. He pulled the curtain back, and Linda could see Isaiah and Tanya walking up the sidewalk.

"Isaiah seems so peaceful," Eric mused. "Sometimes I wish I had decided to become a preacher. Maybe I would be more humble."

Linda got up and joined him at the window. She put her hand on Eric's shoulder. "The grass isn't always greener, Baby. Isaiah has his own problems. He just doesn't know it yet."

Eric turned back to her. "What are you talking about?"

"Just what I said. Your brother has problems, and so does that sister of yours. Dee Dee thinks she has everyone fooled by hanging all over Drake, but mark my words, that marriage is in trouble."

"They look happy enough," Eric said, stepping away from the window. "A whole lot happier than we have been these last few years."

"Well, they're not happy," Linda insisted. "I know you all think I'm just a drunken outsider, but I see things."

Seven

Isaiah lay in bed facing the wall. His eyes were open, but he was dreaming nonetheless. In his mind's eye, he saw himself standing behind the pulpit, delivering his first sermon as senior pastor. Telling his congregation about the love of God and His ability to forgive sins, and the people responding.

When Isaiah finished his sermon, he remained behind the pulpit as hundreds of people jumped out of their seats and ran toward the altar, their faces reflecting the burdens lifted as they cried tears of regret and then joy.

Isaiah pulled the covers back, got out of bed, and fell on his knees. He prayed, "God, was that a vision from You? Will those people still give their lives to You, even if I don't take the senior pastor position?"

Isaiah waited for a response from the Lord, but there was only silence. He stayed on the floor, whispering prayers to the Lord. Tanya was still asleep, so he tried to be as quiet as possible, but he needed direction from God. "Help me, Lord. I don't want to go against Your will, but I need to hear clearly that this is what You want for my life, not just what I want."

Tanya stirred. She lifted her head and looked around. When her eyes spotted Isaiah, she laid her head back on her pillow. "How long have you been up?"

Isaiah had asked Tanya countless times not to interrupt him while he prayed, unless it was an emergency. But Tanya continued to interrupt him whenever she felt like it. He got off his knees and climbed back in bed. "I've been up for a little while."

She yawned and stretched. "What's wrong? Why are you up so early?"

Should he tell her? Would she understand his need to do God's will? When they were engaged, Tanya had acted as if she wanted nothing more than to do the will of God herself. But then, once they got married, and Tanya gave birth to Erin, things changed. She began to fight him about church attendance and anything that had to do with faith in God. Two years ago, she finally told him that if he became pastor of a church, she would leave him.

"I just needed to talk with God about a few things," he said.

Tanya touched his arm. "Is this about that job at the church?"

She said "job" as if Isaiah had applied to become a janitor in an elementary school. He sighed. "No. This is about my ministry and where God wants me."

Tanya scooted closer to him. She was wearing a clingy white silk gown with spaghetti straps. "I don't want to fight with you, Isaiah. I thought we were going to enjoy ourselves this week and not talk about that job."

"I know we agreed to that. But God just showed me a vision of things to come in my ministry."

Tanya put her finger against his mouth. "Let's talk about it later. I think I'd rather talk about this baby you want us to have."

That got his attention. They'd been married seven years, and so far, their efforts at having a second baby had been unsuccessful. The first time had been a fluke. She'd gotten pregnant on their honeymoon when they weren't even trying. And now, they had been trying to conceive for four years, to no avail. Isaiah had asked Tanya to go with him to see a specialist in hopes of determining if either of them had developed a problem that was now making them infertile, but she wouldn't do it.

"You want me to make the doctor's appointment for us?" he asked hopefully.

"No," she said, snuggling up to him. "I think we can handle this on our own."

"Oh," he said, right before the vision from God slipped from his mind.

Shawn's dad had a prayer room in each house he owned. All his kids knew that he could be found in his prayer room every morning before breakfast and every night before he went to bed. And it was an unspoken rule that no one was to disturb him while he was in this room. So, Shawn stood outside of his father's prayer room, waiting for him to finish.

"Hey, Son. Have you been waiting out here long?" Joel asked when he finally opened the door and came out.

"Naw, Dad." Shawn shoved his hands in his pockets. "Just a few minutes."

"You ready for breakfast?"

Shawn wanted to ask his father to go back into his prayer room and pray for him. Right now he desperately needed prayer. He was so confused, he just didn't know what to do. But when he opened his mouth, he simply said, "Yeah, I'm kind of hungry."

Joel laughed as they walked toward the dining room. "I remember how you used to hang out in front of my prayer room when you were a child. You used to wait for me so we could go in to breakfast together. I miss those days."

"I did that a lot, didn't I?"

"If I remember correctly, you walked me into the breakfast room only when you wanted to tell on one of your brothers or sisters. So, who did something this time?" Joel asked with a hint of amusement in his voice.

Shawn stopped walking and lowered his head.

"What's wrong, Son?"

Shawn lifted his head and looked at his father, his eyes filling with tears. "I need to tell on myself this time, Dad. But I'm too much of a coward to rat on myself."

Joel pulled him into an embrace. Shawn's arms went around his dad. When they pulled apart, Joel said, "Whatever it is, Son, your family is here for you."

"Give me a little time, Dad. I thought I could tell you this morning, but I just can't talk about it."

Joel put his hand on Shawn's shoulder and squeezed. "I'm here when you're ready, Son."

"Thanks, Dad. I appreciate that. Let's just go eat for now. Okay?"

After breakfast, the entire family gathered in the media and game room to watch several of Joel's old movies. Lunch was served there afterward, and then they played pool, Monopoly, and table tennis. So far, Elaine had been undefeated in table tennis. Shawn was her last victim, and he was giving her a hard way to go.

Shawn slammed down the Ping-Pong ball on Elaine's side so hard that she couldn't knock it back over to him. "Now what, Little Sis? You think you're bad. I told you, girl, you are up against a real athlete now." Shawn kept selling his wolf tickets.

"I'm not afraid of you, Shawn," Elaine told him. "This is not the football field, and you are going down."

"That's right, sis, you get him," Isaiah said as he walked over to the table.

"Oh, no you don't. Shawn, wipe the table with her," Dee Dee said as she joined them.

Eric laughed and came over to join them. "Looks like I'm going to have to referee this match to make sure everything is on the up-and-up."

"Yeah, come on over, Eric," Shawn said. "Elaine is going to need to cry on her big brother's shoulder when this game is over."

Game was set for the score of seven. So far, Shawn had six points, Elaine four. The ball traveled back and forth between the two. A lot of trash talk went back and forth, and then Elaine scored. She turned to Isaiah. "You must be praying for me."

He grinned. "I certainly am. I don't want this bully to brag about beating a girl."

"Don't you worry," Shawn said. "When I'm done whupping on her, I'll gladly take you on, Big Brother. Then I'll be able to say I can beat men and women."

Tanya came over and stood next to Isaiah. "Keep praying, Honey," she told him. "I want Elaine to smash that ball in Shawn's face."

Shawn scowled at Tanya, and in that moment, Elaine seized her opportunity and hit the ball in his direction. By the time he turned back, he'd missed the ball, and the point went to Elaine.

"The game is now six to six," Eric announced. "The next point will determine the winner."

Dee Dee shoved Shawn. "Watch the table, Boy. What are you doing?"

"Yeah, watch the table, Boy," Elaine taunted.

"Oh, I'm watching, so bring it on." Shawn bent his knees, positioning himself to hit the ball.

They volleyed back and forth, neither willing to relent. Elaine maintained focus until she heard her dad say, "Hey, Elaine. Look who came all the way to the Bahamas to see you."

Elaine hit the ball back to Shawn, looked up, and dropped her paddle just as Shawn hit the ball back to her. "John! What are you doing here?"

He pulled an envelope out of his jacket pocket—her letter. "I came to talk to you about this."

"I won! I won! I won!" Shawn yelled exultantly.

But Elaine no longer cared about winning a silly game. She was too busy thinking about how much she had lost in life as she walked toward the man she so desperately wanted to have and to hold.

They walked on the beach, hand in hand. At times, Elaine rested her head on John's shoulder, put her arm around him, and made other shows of affection. She knew this would be her last moment of normal with the man she loved.

"I don't get it, Elaine. Why would you send a letter breaking off our engagement when you're still in love with me?"

She sat down in the sand and gazed out at the ocean. "Isn't this beach lovely? I've always enjoyed it here. The water is so clear, you can see right to the bottom."

John sat down next to her and reached out, cupping her cheek and turning her face toward him. Looking into her eyes, he asked, "Why do you keep changing the subject? I need to know what's going on."

Elaine blinked back tears. "Let's not talk about that until later. Can we just enjoy what we have right now?"

"I don't understand why you won't tell me what's wrong."

"I will, I promise. Just give me today."

John wiped the tears from her face and gently kissed her. "Okay, Hon, we'll do it your way."

Eight

The next morning, the family gathered in the foyer, ready for a day of sightseeing. Dee Dee noticed that Elaine and John were missing, as was their father. "Didn't John spend the night in the guest room?" she asked of no one in particular.

"Yeah," Shawn confirmed. "Dad made him cancel his hotel reservation."

"Well then, where is he? And where are Elaine and Dad?"

"They're all in Dad's prayer room," Linda spoke up. "I saw them go in there when I was coming downstairs."

Dee Dee nudged Drake. "Now do you believe me? Elaine is up to something. Acting like she was surprised to see John…give me a break."

"You realize you are quite paranoid, right?" Eric said. "There's medication for that, you know."

Dee Dee rolled her eyes. "Laugh if you want, but I'm not about to stand around and watch Little Miss Buttercup pray her way into my inheritance. I'm going to see what they're doing."

"Why don't we just wait until they're done, and then we can all leave together?" Drake suggested.

"I will not! I'm going in that prayer room."

"Don't interrupt Dad, Dee Dee," Shawn said.

"Shut up, Shawn. Just because you spent your childhood lurking around Daddy's prayer room, afraid to go in, doesn't mean the rest of us are." She marched out of the foyer, ignoring the protests of her husband and brothers. Heading down the hallway, she kept mumbling, "I'm not going to let Elaine's slick fiancé steal what belongs to me." She knocked on the door. When no one responded, Dee Dee knocked again and then said, "Daddy, it's me. Open the door."

By the time her father opened the door, Drake and Isaiah had come, too, and were trying to get Dee Dee to go with them. But she refused to budge.

Her father had tears in his eyes. "Can you all give us a few more minutes?"

Now Dee Dee was really curious. "Why are you crying, Daddy?" She kept her hand on the doorknob.

Gently, her father pried Dee Dee's fingers off the knob. "Why don't you all go on with your sightseeing? When you get back, we can have dinner together."

"Is everything okay, Dad?" Isaiah sounded concerned.

"We'll talk about it this evening, Son." With that, Joel closed the door and locked it.

Dee Dee turned to Isaiah. "What do you suppose that was all about?"

Isaiah grabbed her arm and pulled her down the hall. Drake followed behind them. "I don't know," Isaiah said, "but I think we should do exactly what Dad asked us to do."

Dee Dee rolled her eyes but kept walking. When they were back in the foyer, Eric raised his eyebrows at her. "So, did you satisfy your curiosity?"

"Absolutely not. Daddy wouldn't tell me a thing."

"Your father did ask that we all go sightseeing without them," Drake told him. "They'll join us for dinner tonight."

"Is Joel not feeling well?" Tanya asked.

"He was certainly crying, so something has to be wrong," Dee Dee said, stepping away from the group. "You all can go. I'm staying here until I find out exactly what's going on."

"Why was Dad crying?" Shawn asked.

"We don't know," Isaiah said, "but I think he wants some time alone with Elaine and John. So, let's just go sightseeing."

Dee Dee shook her head. "If he wanted to be alone with Elaine and John, he shouldn't have invited all of us here. This just isn't fair."

Eyes rolling heavenward, Linda exclaimed, "You are such a drama queen!"

Dee Dee glared at her. "This is none of your business. Why don't you just go get a drink and let me talk to my family?"

Drake raised his hands. "Look, we agreed to go sightseeing today, so let's just do it. All right?"

Dee Dee let out a loud huff but went along with the group.

Inside his prayer room, Joel felt as if his heart was breaking into irreparable pieces. Elaine had asked him and John to sit down so she could talk to them. He'd thought she was going to tell them that she didn't want a big wedding, that she couldn't deal with spending all that money on a gown, flowers, and a caterer. Joel had been prepared to hear his kindhearted daughter say that she wanted to have the pastor marry her at home, so that he could donate the money she would have spent on the wedding to a worthy cause. But that wasn't what Elaine had said.

Standing before Joel and her fiancé with her hands clasped in front of her, Elaine had hesitated for a moment, taken a deep breath, and then turned to Joel and said, "John came here this week because he wants to know why I called off our wedding."

Completely confused, Joel had turned from Elaine to John and then back again. "Called off the wedding? What happened? What's wrong?"

"That's what I've been trying to find out," John had said.

Elaine had looked from Joel to John, her eyes shining with compassion. "I'm sorry if it seems inconsiderate of me to tell you this at the same time." Her voice had broken as fresh tears had trickled down her face. "But I didn't want to go through this twice."

John had stood up and wrapped his arms around Elaine. "What is it, Honey? Why are you so upset?"

Elaine had laid her head on John's shoulder and cried. They'd clung to one another until Joel had gotten to his feet, as well. "You're scaring me, Elaine. I need to know what's going on."

Elaine had pulled away from John and wiped the tears from her face. She'd pointed at the seats Joel and John had vacated. "Can you please sit back down?"

"Just go ahead and tell us, Buttercup," Joel had urged her. "It can't be that bad."

Another tear had rolled down Elaine's cheek, and she'd wiped it away. "I'd rather that you and John sit down. Okay, Dad?"

They'd done as asked. Elaine hadn't hesitated this time; she'd opened her mouth and said, "I hadn't been feeling well for a little while, so I went to the doctor, and after he ran several tests, he discovered that I have"—she'd taken a deep breath before finishing—"ovarian cancer."

Joel had tried to stand, but his wobbly legs wouldn't hold him, so he'd fallen back in his seat. "No, that's not possible!" He'd stood back up and rushed to Elaine's side. "What doctor said this to you?" Looking back now, Joel realized it had sounded as if he was planning to confront the man and make him change his diagnosis immediately.

It was then that Dee Dee had interrupted them. After she'd gone, Joel had sat back down, stunned. After a few minutes of silence, he asked again, "What doctor diagnosed you?"

"Dr. Perrin."

"Is he the only doctor you've seen?" John's voice sounded calm but concerned.

She nodded.

"Well then, you need a second opinion," Joel told her. "Let's pray, and then I'm going to call a doctor in the States and get you back there immediately."

"Thank you, Dad. I know this is a tough thing for you to go through, especially after losing your other children all those years ago. I apologize for not getting to the doctor sooner."

"Hush with that, Buttercup. We're going to get you to a specialist and get this thing taken care of. You've got many years left to live," Joel said with confidence.

"I hope you're right, but if I don't make it, I need to ask you to do something for me." She held up a hand as both John and her father tried to object. "Just hear me out." She hesitated for a moment but then carried on. "I know that you are supposed to be telling us about changes to your will this weekend. I just wanted to ask you to start a foundation for missionaries with my portion."

Joel walked over to his daughter and wrapped his arms around her. When they parted, his eyes were filled with tears of love. "You are the most generous child I have. We will start that foundation for missionaries while you are alive, and you and John will be the first recipients."

Elaine turned tearful eyes to John, who nodded.

"Okay, Daddy." She sniffled. "John and I will do missionary work together again, I promise you. But there's one last thing."

Joel sat down, fearing that his heart would give out if his child revealed any more bad news. "What is it?"

"I can't check myself into the hospital until I know that Natua will be provided for."

John put a hand on Elaine's shoulder. "I think it's best if we get you to a doctor right away."

"I understand that, John, but I can't abandon Natua." She turned to Joel, her face imploring him to help her. "I will go to the hospital and do whatever you ask, if you can help me to convince Dee Dee to go to Uganda and adopt Natua."

Nine

Joel didn't know if he would be able to pull off Elaine's request. He knew his children, and while he loved each of them, he wasn't blind to their faults. Where Elaine was sometimes too generous, Dee Dee was almost always selfish. When she was a child, Joel had indulged her behavior. His wife had warned him that he would come to regret letting that girl have her way so often. He just hoped that today wouldn't be that day.

As everyone sat around the table after dinner, enjoying a dessert of apple pie Mary had baked, Joel decided to take charge. He stood up, and the group quieted down as everyone turned in his direction. They had expectant looks on their faces, as if they'd known something was coming and had been on pins and needles for some time.

He cleared his throat. "I was going to wait until tomorrow after breakfast to discuss the changes to my will; but something has come up, and Elaine and I will be leaving first thing in the morning. So, I figured now is as good a time as any." He took a deep breath. "I've instructed my lawyer to change my will so that ninety percent of my assets will go to charity."

Dee Dee dropped her fork. "You must be joking."

"No, Honey, I'm not." He looked around the room, his eyes scanning the faces of the sons and daughters he was so proud of. "You all have done so much for yourselves that you hardly need my money to survive. The ten percent that will be split among all of you will be more than enough."

"Isaiah and I don't make that much money," Tanya quickly interjected. "I mean, he's just a lowly assistant pastor. He doesn't make movies, play pro football, or run a city."

Isaiah covered Tanya's hand with his. "Dad, don't worry about it," he said. "We're okay with whatever you decide to do with your money."

Tanya snatched her hand away from him. "Speak for yourself," she snarled. "I'm not okay with this at all. Your father should be thinking about his family rather than some obscure charity cases."

"Oh, shut up, Tanya," Dee Dee put in. "This is none of your business, anyway."

In a huff, Tanya stood up and slammed her chair against the table. "It is just as much my business as any of yours. If you all are going to sit here and pretend that you're okay with this"—she pointed an accusatory finger in Joel's direction—"and that this man doesn't need a mental competency hearing, I'm not going to be a part of this."

Linda looked at Tanya and laughed.

Tanya folded her arms across her chest. "I don't see what's so funny."

"And I don't see why you're so upset. You're sleeping with Shawn, so why don't you just ask him for some money?"

Eric pulled his wife to her feet. "Let's go. I knew that wasn't just iced tea that you were sipping on all day long. And I saw you mix that vodka in your orange juice this morning."

Linda wriggled away from him. "I'm not drunk," she insisted. "I saw Shawn sneaking into Tanya's bedroom when Isaiah was at the beach with the kids."

The entire room erupted.

"What are you talking about?" Isaiah demanded.

"She doesn't know what she's saying, Isaiah," Eric hastened to say. "I'm sorry, but my wife is sick."

"Ask him!" Linda shouted, pointing at Shawn. "He'll tell you it's true."

Shawn sat silently with his head lowered.

"I knew she was no good." Dee Dee shook her head at Tanya. "How could you sleep with two brothers?"

Drake frowned. "Hush up, Dee Dee. This isn't our business."

"What's wrong, Drake? Did she sleep with you, too? Oh, never mind. I forgot—you're too good and godly to do something like that, right?" Dee Dee sneered at him.

Linda glared at Dee Dee. "And why don't the two of you stop the charade and just admit that you don't like each other?"

Everyone looked at Shawn, waiting for him to respond.

Finally, Isaiah shouted, "Say something, Shawn!"

Joel raised his hands. "Okay, I need everyone to sit and calm down. We have more to discuss."

But no one was listening. Dee Dee was shouting at Linda, Linda was shouting at Tanya, and Isaiah was trying to talk to his wife.

Finally Elaine stood up and yelled at the top of her lungs, "I have cancer!"

Ten

The room became deathly silent as everyone stared at Elaine.

"I'm sorry," she murmured. "I didn't mean to blurt it out like that, but you all were getting so riled up, and I need help right now."

"How can you have cancer?" Dee Dee asked. "You're only twenty-four." For a change, her tone wasn't accusatory; it was sad and frightened.

Elaine shrugged her shoulders. "I wish I knew."

Isaiah came around the table and put his arms around Elaine. "This is not a death sentence for you. We are going to pray and believe that God will allow you to be healed."

"Thanks, Isaiah. I would like that very much."

Joel cleared his throat again. "Can everyone please sit back down, so I can finish this?"

For the moment, the group seemed to have forgotten about Linda's accusations against Shawn and Tanya, and Dee Dee and Drake. They returned to their seats and looked at him expectantly.

"The floor is yours," Eric told him.

Joel nodded. "While I had contemplated giving ninety percent of my money to charity, my conversation with Elaine changed my mind."

"Thank God for that," Dee Dee said.

"Elaine has such a giving heart that I truly believe God is going to bless her and see her through this dark time in her life." He cast a loving gaze around the table. "But I want to give all of you the opportunity to understand that simple Bible verse that says, '*It is more blessed to give than to receive.*' So, I'm asking each of you to start a foundation and give the money away yourself." He said this as if he expected his children to jump for joy any minute.

They all looked at each other, as if searching for the punch line, and then Shawn spoke up. "So, we don't get to have any of the money for ourselves?"

"You'll each get about ten million from my estate when I'm dead and gone," Joel said, "but I want you to work on your foundations now. It would do my heart good to see my children blessing others. Elaine has already designated that a foundation for missionaries be set up in her honor. So, what do you say? Can you all do this for your old man?"

Isaiah and Shawn silently nodded their acceptance, while Eric made no response.

Dee Dee rolled her eyes. "I'm telling you right now, I'm not doing this at all—not unless I can at least retain the interest that money will earn while I'm trying to figure out which charity to give it to." She said "give" as if it was a dirty word.

"That sounds fair to me, especially since I need to ask you and Drake for another favor," Joel said.

Dee Dee sneered. "You strip us of our birthright, and I'm now supposed to do you a favor on top of it? Give me a break."

"Don't talk to your father like that," Drake whispered to his wife.

Dee Dee turned her scorn on her husband. "Don't you say another word to me. It's clear that I didn't need you this weekend, after all." She turned back to her father. "Just so you know, Daddy, as soon as I get back home, I'm divorcing Drake."

Drake clasped his hands together and leaned back in his seat. His lips were pressed tightly together, as if he were trying to stop certain words from escaping his mouth.

Linda nudged Eric. "I told you."

"Shut up, Linda," Dee Dee spat. "Just go get yourself another drink."

Joel looked heavenward. "Lord, how much prayer will be enough?" He then turned pitying eyes on his daughter. "I'm sorry to hear that, Dee Dee. I hope you'll change your mind, especially since your sister needs you right now."

Dee Dee bit her lip. "Just because I'm upset with you doesn't mean I won't help my sister," she finally said. "I will help Elaine in whatever way she needs."

"I'm glad to hear you say that," Elaine replied. "As you know, I have been taking care of a little girl named Natua. But I don't know how long my recovery process will be, so I need you to go to Uganda and get her."

"Okay, that's not a problem." Dee Dee shrugged. "Where do I take her once I bring her back here?"

"To your house. I want you to adopt her."

Epilogue

The doctors weren't optimistic about Elaine's chances. After several tests had been completed, it was determined that her cancer was in the final stage. The best doctor Joel could find had only recommended chemotherapy. But even he admitted that it probably wouldn't do much good.

John entered Elaine's hospital room one day carrying a huge book. "We're going to Mexico," he said, setting the book down in front of her.

"What are you talking about, John? I'm in the hospital. I can't just get up and go to Mexico." She glanced at the book cover and read the words "Gerson Institute."

"I'm talking about the Gerson Therapy for healing cancer," John said. "I've read all about it, Elaine, and I think we need to give it a try."

Elaine put her hand over John's. She really loved this man, but she would not allow him to sit around waiting for something that wouldn't happen. "I'm dying, John. You need to get on with your life."

He shook his head. "You *are* my life, and I'm not going anywhere."

She gave a bitter laugh. "I can't say the same thing. You've heard the doctors. Why are you still hanging around?"

Ignoring her, he continued. "I talked with your dad about this clinic in Mexico. He agrees with me that we should give it a try. Our flight leaves in two days…right after you marry me."

Elaine closed her eyes. From the day she met John, she'd wanted nothing more than to marry this man and spend the rest of her days with him. But her life expectancy was too short. "I can't marry you, John. I wish things were different."

"Okay then, if you want things to be different, then come to Mexico with me. Give yourself a chance to live, so that you *can* marry me."

Tears ran down her face as she summoned the courage to hope. She'd almost given up and simply accepted that her life would soon be over. But the love she saw in John's eyes gave her the strength to believe again. Maybe God wasn't done with her yet.

She nodded. "I'll go with you, my love."

John leaned over and kissed her. "And you'll live, and we'll marry."

The Wild One

One

Leaving me isn't going to be as easy as you think. I'm not like the others.

Dee Dee Morrison-Wilcox-Johnson-Sooner-Milner rolled her eyes as she read the e-mail. She didn't recognize the sender's address, but it had to be Drake Milner, her soon-to-be ex-husband.

Drake was husband number four. When they'd first gotten married, Dee Dee had thought that Drake was the love of her life and that all those previous marriages had been foolish detours on her way to her happily ever after. But Drake was too much like Dee Dee's father, the great Joel Morrison. She would have divorced him already if it weren't for sweet little Natua.

Natua had lost both her parents before her second birthday. Dee Dee's sister, Elaine, who had been a missionary in Uganda, began helping the girl's grandmother take care of her. Elaine had fallen in love with the little girl, and Natua loved her, also. So, Elaine had started to think about adopting her. But then, Elaine had been diagnosed with ovarian cancer. Now Dee Dee's little sister was in a fight for her life, and she had asked Dee Dee to adopt Natua.

Dee Dee had not been at all prepared for Elaine's proposition. She'd never wanted children. Her first inclination was to decline—not just say "No" but "Absolutely not!" But, after her father went on to explain that her sister refused to get treatment unless she knew that Natua was safe, Dee Dee began thinking about how in vogue it could be to adopt a girl from Africa. After all, celebrities adopted children from other countries all the time. Just look at Angelina Jolie and Sandra Bullock. Doing something like this could really help her career—maybe even take it to the next level.

Her agent and the producers on her sitcom had congratulated her. They'd even offered to do a press release about the adoption. But Dee Dee had said no to the press release, because she didn't want any reporters getting wind of Elaine's illness and then tracking her down in Mexico, where she was currently seeking treatment.

Drake had agreed to help her with the child, and so far, their arrangement was working out just fine. Drake kept Natua three days a week—Tuesday, Wednesday, and Friday—the days that Dee Dee was needed on the set to film her latest sitcom.

Dee Dee and Drake had agreed that he should stay at Dee Dee's house on the days he was responsible for Natua, to spare the girl a constant change of scenery. They figured she had endured more than enough instances of uprooting in her young life. That didn't bother Dee Dee, because she left the house at five in the morning and didn't return home until nightfall. But these love notes Drake kept sending her were really beginning to bug her.

She walked into Natua's room. "You ready, Kiddo?"

"Yep." Natua slipped on her pink tennis shoes. "Will Daddy be here this morning to tie my laces?"

"No, Honey. Remember, Drake likes to stay at his apartment on Thursdays."

"Oh, yeah." Natua nodded. "And on Saturday, and Sunday, and Monday, too. Daddy likes being alone a lot."

It bugged Dee Dee that after three months, Natua already thought of Drake as *Daddy* but still couldn't bring herself to call Dee Dee "Mommy." But Dee Dee also realized that Natua had thought of Elaine as her new mommy and had expected to live with her, until Dee Dee showed up. Elaine wasn't married, and so, not having grown accustomed to calling another man "Daddy," Natua had attached herself easily to Drake. Dee Dee knew this in her head, but her heart was having a hard time accepting it—especially since she had begun thinking of Natua as her very own child and wouldn't dream of giving her up, not even to Elaine, assuming she pulled through her illness.

Dee Dee smiled at the innocent little girl. "Let me tie your shoes so we can get going."

Dee Dee didn't need to be on the set today, but she had a meeting with her agent about a movie role she was interested in. The role she would be playing was very different from the Pollyanna, good-girl roles she had been typecast in. At first, Dee Dee hadn't minded doing family-oriented movies. After all, her father had made his money starring in family-friendly movies. But the Hollywood of today was very different from the days when Joel Morrison had risen to stardom.

Dee Dee was a C-list star, reduced to playing secondary characters on sitcoms because she'd never had the guts to take risks with her career. But this new script would bring Pollyanna out of the box and catapult her career in viewer-discretion-advised arenas. And that would be huge.

Natua jumped up and put her hands on her hips. "What'ya think?"

This had become their daily ritual. Natua wanted to know how she looked in all of her pretty new clothes.

Dee Dee smiled down at the precious girl in her terrycloth dress. "I think you're beautiful. Lime green is definitely your color."

"O-tay, I ready." Natua grabbed Dee Dee's hand and hopped and bounced all the way out the door.

After dropping off Natua at day care, Dee Dee headed to Toscana to meet her agent, Nick Rosenthal, for lunch. As she walked toward their usual table, Dee Dee was reminded of just how gorgeous her agent was. Even so, Nick didn't stand out in the crowd. LA was full of blond white men with plastic smiles.

Nick stood up and kissed Dee Dee on both cheeks. "Beautiful as ever," he said, and then they both took their seats.

"I hope I didn't keep you waiting too long."

"Not at all," Nick said, with that famous plastic smile. "I already ordered for us. I hope you don't mind."

"What did you get me?"

"The grilled Pacific sea bass."

"Perfect."

The waitress arrived at the table with a mineral water for Dee Dee and an iced tea for Nick. "Your meal will be out in a few minutes," she told them, then turned and strode away from their table.

"So, tell me everything," Dee Dee began excitedly. "Has Michael Mavs decided on the actor who'll be playing my love interest yet?"

Nick nodded as he took a sip of his tea.

"Well, spill it! Did he choose Jarrod Lovett, like I suggested?"

"He sure did."

Now Dee Dee was smiling. "I'm absolutely thrilled. Jarrod and I will smoke up the screen. We've always had great chemistry; the roles we've played just didn't allow us to show it."

Nick put his elbows on the table and leaned in closer to Dee Dee. "That's just it…." His words trailed off as the waitress arrived at the table with their food.

She set their plates in front of them and said, "Let me know if you need anything else."

Dee Dee took a bite of her fish and closed her eyes, savoring the flavors that exploded on her tongue. She hated being so predictable with her food choices that her agent could order for her, wherever they dined. But, hey, she liked what she liked. "This is de-lish."

"I knew you'd like it." Nick drummed his fingers on the table. "About Jarrod Lovett. The producers liked him for the male lead. But here's the problem...."

Dee Dee was happily eating her fish, half listening to Nick until now. She looked up from her plate. "Problem? What problem?"

"You know that chemistry you and Jarrod have?"

"Yeah, what about it?"

"He's not so sure. Jarrod has only seen you in very chaste roles, and he doesn't think you can pull off an R-rated film."

Dee Dee's fork fell from her hand and clanged against her plate. "No, he didn't. If it wasn't for me, that little ingrate never would have gotten the role in the last film we appeared in together. I practically gift wrapped this role for him by bragging about him to Michael Mavs like an idiot, and then he goes and stabs me in the back."

Nick held up a hand to silence her. "It sounded like Jarrod was more concerned about what might happen to you and your career if you did a movie like this."

Dee Dee swept her hair back with her hand. "My career is just fine."

"Jarrod seems to believe that you have acquired a niche audience over the years—viewers who don't expect to see Dee Dee Morrison in a skin flick. And, to be honest with you, I can't say I disagree with him. Your regular audience will be disappointed by this role, and if the film flops, your career could be over."

"But if the film is a success, I could be looking at an Oscar. Then directors will offer me bigger roles than the choir girls and do-gooders I've been playing my whole career."

"That is true. But I do think this new role deserves a second thought. I mean, are you really comfortable doing nude scenes? Can you really live with the backlash you'll receive from doing this film?"

Dee Dee wiped her mouth and threw down her napkin. "Are you my agent or my priest? It's not your job to question what roles might be good for my soul. You are supposed to get me the roles I want. That's it and that's all."

Nick raised his hands in surrender. "Hey, you are absolutely right. And that's why I got you a meeting with Michael and Jarrod. They want to speak with you personally and run a couple of lines."

Dee Dee practically spat, "I have to audition for this role?"

Nick squirmed in his seat. "Consider it more like a friendly meet-and-greet."

She scowled. "I already know Michael and Jarrod, and I really don't feel like greeting either one of them right now."

"They want to meet with you at eleven tomorrow morning. Just go and hear them out. Blow them away with your skillful performance as you read the lines. Take off your clothes, if you want; show them how comfortable you are with being nude."

Dee Dee balked. "I wouldn't lower myself to undress for either of those animals. My fans love me. And Michael and Jarrod need to recognize that I have box office success because my audience follows me from movie to movie." She stood up and shoved her chair against the table. "I'll go to that meeting tomorrow, but you let them know that I am not auditioning for anything. You tell them that if they want this film to succeed, then they need to recognize that Dee Dee Morrison is the woman who can make that happen." With that, she turned and stalked out of the restaurant.

Two

After her meeting with Nick, Dee Dee was so angry that she needed some mall therapy. She shopped for hours. She'd intended to shop for herself, but in each store she entered, she ended up in the kids' section, purchasing a dress, a pair of jeans, or an entire outfit for Natua.

At the end of the afternoon, she packed her shopping bags into her Mercedes and drove to the day care to pick up her little princess.

Natua ran to her and gave her a big hug.

After a moment, Dee Dee stepped back and noticed the smudges of dirt covering Natua's dress. "What happened to you?"

"Sorry about that," Natua's teacher spoke up. "She got a little dirty on the playground today."

The first day of school, Natua had worn a pretty pink shirt Dee Dee had purchased for her at an expensive little boutique—and she'd gotten it dirty during playtime. Dee Dee had gone ballistic. The teacher had tried to explain to her that it wasn't uncommon for children to soil their clothes while playing, but Dee Dee hadn't been convinced. She'd been sure there had to be a way to keep children's clothes clean, even on a playground. But, in the weeks that had followed, she had come to accept that children not only attract dirt; they like it.

Natua's antics sometimes reminded Dee Dee of the fun she and Elaine had as children. And she remembered how it drove their mother crazy when she couldn't get spots and stains out of their clothes. Thinking of those times always put a smile on Dee Dee's face. She often found herself wondering why she'd spent so much time resenting Elaine, when she should have just enjoyed the fact that she had a sister. Nothing like an illness in the family to bring perspective.

When they arrived at home, Natua was so excited about her new clothes that she wanted to try everything on as soon as they walked in the door.

"Not so fast, Little One," Dee Dee told her. "First you need to eat. Sit at the table while I make you a ham and cheese sandwich."

"Okay, Dee Dee, but hurry." Natua jumped in her seat as if her pants were on fire and she was trying to squelch the flames.

Dee Dee chuckled and shook her head as she went to the fridge for some lunch meat, cheese, and mustard. Natua liked her ham and cheese sandwiches to be made like grilled cheese—the way Drake made them—and so, not to be outdone, Dee Dee always fixed the girl's sandwiches just the way she liked them. She took out a skillet, sprayed it with Pam, and assembled the sandwich on whole wheat bread, which she then fried.

"Here you go, Honey." Dee Dee plated the sandwich and placed it in front of Natua. She then put the lunch meat and mustard back inside the refrigerator and grabbed a juicy drink. As she closed the refrigerator door, she noticed a piece of paper fall to the floor.

That was odd, because she never hung anything on her refrigerator. She thought that people who did things like that were just plain tacky themselves. She picked up the paper and it.

I don't like Natua in green. She should always wear pink. Make sure she wears the dress I laid on her bed to school tomorrow.

That settled it. Dee Dee was changing the locks on her doors, and Drake would just have to babysit Natua at his own apartment. Who did he think he was, anyway, barging into her house, leaving notes on the refrigerator and clothes on Natua's bed? Drake Milner had lost the right to insert himself into her life when he'd started acting too much like her father, with all of his Bible reading and praying at the drop of a hat. And she was going to tell him just that, as soon as she put Natua to bed.

"You done with your sandwich?"

Natua swallowed and wiped her hands. "Yep."

Dee Dee handed her the juice. "Here. Drink up, and then we can go upstairs and try on your new clothes."

Natua did as she was told, then jumped out of her seat and ran upstairs.

Laughing again, Dee Dee picked up the shopping bags and started up the staircase. Natua wasn't her natural born child, but, day by day, she was acting more like Dee Dee than she cared to admit. "Slow down, Girl. You're going to fall up the stairs."

Natua hollered back, "Hurry up, Dee Dee! I want to see what you bought me."

"I have the stuff in my hands," Dee Dee called up to her. "You won't see it until I get there, so you might as well wait for me."

But Dee Dee's logic fell on deaf ears. She heard Natua race down the hall to her room, giggling all the way. When Dee Dee reached the top of the steps, Natua rushed back to her, wrapped her arms around Dee Dee's waist, and clung to her.

"What's wrong, Honey?"

Natua pointed toward her room. "It's broken."

"Huh? What's broken?" Although Dee Dee was trying to follow their conversation, she still had a lot of problems with three-year-old speak.

"My room," Natua sobbed. "Somebody tore it up."

Dee Dee plied Natua's hands from around her waist as she rushed down the hall toward the little girl's room. When she reached the door, Dee Dee was startled by what she saw. Clothes were strewn all over the floor. Certain items had been ripped apart, and others were almost shredded. She dropped the bags as she put her hand over mouth and stepped into the room. *Who would do something like this?* She bent down and started picking up torn dresses and shirts.

"Don't be sad, Dee Dee," Natua said. She came into the room and picked up a few shirts off the floor. "Look, my pink shirts are fine."

Dee Dee's head popped up as Natua held out the pink shirts to her. Then she remembered the note on her refrigerator and turned toward Natua's bed. A pink shirt and a mauve pair of pants lay on top of the bedspread. Dee Dee straightened and took Natua's hand, leading her out of the room. "Let's go back downstairs."

Natua pulled back, grabbing one of the bags that Dee Dee had dropped in front of the bedroom door. "Don't forget my new clothes, Dee Dee. They might get torn up, too."

Dee Dee grabbed the other bags and then ushered the little girl back downstairs, where she grabbed her purse and car keys, then rushed out of the house with Natua and her new clothes. Someone had been in her home, and Dee Dee knew now that it hadn't been Drake. Her faithful Christian husband would never do something so cruel to sweet little Natua.

She threw the shopping bags and her purse in the passenger door, buckled Natua into her car seat, got in the driver's seat, and then locked the doors before putting the key in the ignition. Natua started crying and squirming in her seat. "We're just going for a little drive," Dee Dee told her as she backed out of the driveway.

"I want Daddy."

Come to think of it, calling Drake wouldn't be a bad idea. "Okay, Honey. Let's call Daddy." Dee Dee pulled the car to the side of the road and reached in her purse for her cell phone. When Drake answered, she didn't waste time with small talk. "Drake, someone's been in the house. Natua's room has been torn apart. What are you doing? Can you come over?"

"Slow down. What are you talking about?"

"Drake, we need you. Please come to the house. Natua is very upset."

"I'm on my way."

Dee Dee hit the end button and threw her cell phone back in her purse. She leaned back to wipe the tears from Natua's face. "Daddy's on his way. Everything's going to be all right, you'll see."

"Daddy's gon' punch 'em in the face for tearing up my clothes," Natua said, balling up her hands into tiny fists and swiping at the air.

Dee Dee wanted to tell Natua that she might as well give up her dreams of seeing a fight. Drake would more likely get on his knees and pray for the soul of the intruder. Shaking her head, Dee Dee wondered for the hundredth time how someone as fine and sexy as Drake Milner could be as rigid as Moses carrying the Ten Commandments. "How about we go get some ice cream while we wait for Daddy to get here?"

A loud cheer came from the backseat as Dee Dee pulled off. If traffic was decent, it would still take Drake about thirty minutes to get to the house. The ice cream shop was just down the street, so Dee Dee knew they had time to go there and get back before Drake arrived.

And that's what she did. By the time Drake pulled his Range Rover next to her car, Dee Dee and Natua were happily finishing their vanilla and chocolate swirl ice cream cones. The car door was still locked, just in case whoever had ransacked Natua's room decided to bum-rush them while they were enjoying their ice cream. She unlocked the doors, and Drake helped Natua out of her car seat.

"Daddy, Daddy, I knew you'd come." Natua wrapped her arms around his neck.

"You didn't have to worry about that, Hon. Now let's go check out your room."

Natua shook her head furiously. "I don't want my room anymore, Daddy. It's broken."

Drake glanced over at Dee Dee and silently communicated his concern. "I'll fix it for you, Baby. It'll be like new."

They entered the house, and Dee Dee stayed in the foyer with Natua while Drake went upstairs to survey the situation. When he came back down, he was carrying several garments that had been ripped apart. "Who would do this to a child?" he demanded.

"I don't know. At first, I thought it was you."

"Me?" He held up the torn clothes. "What in the world would make you think I would do something like this?"

"I didn't think you destroyed Natua's room. I've been receiving these e-mails, and then there was a note on the refrigerator. I thought you had sent those notes, but once I entered Natua's room, I knew you had nothing to do with it."

"What notes?"

Dee Dee walked into the kitchen, Drake and Natua trailing her. She grabbed the note and handed it to Drake.

After reading it, he said, "Call the police."

"But, Drake, if I call the police, it will be all over the news and on entertainment television," Dee Dee protested. "And you know as well as I do that if producers find out that I have a stalker, they'll put me on the bubonic plague list."

"This isn't about your career, Dee Dee. Whoever this guy is, he has been spying on Natua. We have to protect her. I'm going to check this house from top to bottom, and if you haven't called the police by the time I finish, I will."

"Get the baseball bat from the garage," Dee Dee suggested. "If he's still in here, you'll need something to knock him out with."

"I've got all I need with me right now."

Dee Dee didn't see any weapon in Drake's hand. "What do you have?"

He responded, "Holy Ghost power."

Murmuring under her breath, Dee Dee marched to the garage to grab the bat.

"All clear," Drake said after scouring the house. "Did you call the police?"

"Well, no, I was hoping that you'd find him in the house, and then we'd beat the living daylights out of him."

Drake picked up the telephone and dialed 9-1-1. When the operator came on the line, he told her about the situation and then gave her the address.

When he hung up the phone, he turned to Dee Dee. She was leaning against the wall with her arms folded across her chest.

"I guess you're mad at me."

She shook her head. "No, you're right. It's one thing to stalk me, but this nut obviously has also been stalking Natua. We need to do something about this."

Drake stared at her for a moment, then turned away. "The first thing we need to do is pray."

Rolling her eyes, Dee Dee unfolded her arms and moved away from the wall. "Instead of getting on your knees, you need to learn how to ball up your fist. Or, better yet, go buy a gun. Natua and I don't need a prayer warrior. We need a man who can take care of business."

Ignoring her taunts, Drake headed for the room in the back of the house that had been his prayer sanctuary when he'd lived there.

She went into the family room and sat next to Natua on the sofa. "Well, Natua, it looks like you and I are going to be the ones balling up our fists."

"Daddy can fight, too."

"No, Baby, Daddy doesn't like to fight. He prefers to pray."

"I'm going to pray with him." Natua stood up and scampered down the hall to Drake's prayer room.

"Guess I'm the only one in this family that's willing to put up my dukes and go to battle," she muttered to herself.

The doorbell rang. Still shaking her head in disgust, Dee Dee went to see who it was. She peeked through the window and saw two police officers standing on the front porch. She opened the door and welcomed them inside.

"We received a call about a home invasion," one of the officers said.

"Yes." Dee Dee nodded. "Let me show you my daughter's room." She showed the officers upstairs. "This is how I found the room when I arrived home this afternoon. We moved a couple of the outfits, but everything is just about the way it was."

The taller of the two police officers looked around the room, scribbled something in a notebook, and then asked, "Were any other rooms disturbed?"

"No, but he left a note for me on the refrigerator."

"Do you still have it?" the shorter police officer asked.

Dee Dee noticed that the shorter officer had startlingly gorgeous green eyes and a face to match. LA was full of beautiful people, but most of them couldn't act and had to find other work. "Yes. Let me take you to the kitchen where I left it."

In the kitchen, Dee Dee found Drake at the stove fixing Ramen Noodles—or, as Natua called them, "perfect" noodles. The child had access to the finest cuisine that Los Angeles had to offer, but she preferred Ramen Noodles over penne or linguine. Dee Dee didn't understand it one bit.

"Here it is," Dee Dee said, handing the note to Officer Beautiful.

He took the note and read it. "So, you think that the person who wrote this note also left that pink outfit on the bed upstairs?"

"I do."

"Okay. Well, we'll take that outfit and this note to see if we can get any prints off of them. Is there anything else?"

Dee Dee walked over to the kitchen table and sat down in front of her laptop. "I received an e-mail a few days ago. At first, I thought my husband had sent it, but now I'm not so sure." She booted up the computer, opened her Outlook file, and clicked on the message.

Drake and the officers stepped up behind her to read over her shoulder.

Leaving me isn't going to be as easy as you think.
I'm not like the others.

"You thought I sent an e-mail like that to you?" Drake asked incredulously.

"Drake, can we please stick to the issue at hand?" She turned her attention back to the police officers. "I don't know why this guy is fixated on me or why he's so interested in Natua's wardrobe, but I need him to stop."

"We'll do everything we can." The taller officer handed Dee Dee a business card. "Please forward that e-mail to the address printed on this card."

"We'll be in touch," Officer Beautiful said, after they'd collected everything. They headed to the front door.

Drake walked them out. When he came back to the kitchen, he took the noodles out of the pot, cut them up in a bowl, and served them to a smiling Natua. "Eat up, Hon. I'm going to talk with Dee Dee for a minute, and then I'll be back in here to check on you, okay?"

"All right, Daddy." Natua began slurping noodles and seemed to forget all about the turmoil.

Drake followed Dee Dee into the living room. "I'm not leaving you alone and defenseless," he told her. "I'm moving back in until we figure out who this maniac is and what he really wants."

Dee Dee planted her hands on her hips. "Absolutely not. Natua and I will be fine now that we're in the house. I do have an alarm system, remember?"

"And yet, somehow, this guy was able to get in the house anyway."

"I just don't think that it's necessary to change our living arrangements."

"I don't care what you think, Dee. I'm not leaving the two of you alone, and that's final." Drake walked back into the kitchen, leaving Dee Dee standing with her mouth hanging open.

Three

Standing on the balcony, Dee Dee watched the palm trees sway in the breeze. She inhaled the salty fragrance of sea water and exhaled. She felt good here…like she had finally done the right thing.

"Come back to bed, Baby."

She smiled. His voice was like slow jazz on a warm summer night. He meant everything to her, and she owed her father a world of thanks for introducing them. "I'll be in soon. This breeze just feels so good."

He got out of bed and sauntered over to her, pulling her into his arms and nibbling on her neck. "You feel good. Come on, I can't get to sleep without you by my side."

Dee Dee laughed. "I know you, Husband. You aren't really thinking about sleep."

He kissed her ear this time, and then her neck, and then her shoulder. "Come back to bed and find out."

She allowed him to pull her back inside. In bed again, he began to kiss her hungrily. Dee Dee was swept away. Love didn't usually make her emotional, but he made her feel things she had never experienced before. She opened her mouth and screamed his name….

Dee Dee shot up in her bed and clamped her hand over her mouth. She looked around, making sure she was alone. Why she had been dreaming about their honeymoon, she couldn't begin to comprehend. The resort had been beautiful and exotic, and she and Drake had truly been at peace there. But the moment they'd returned home, he'd gotten on her case about attending church and praying with him. When they'd first married, Dee Dee thought that the fourth time had to be the charm, but Drake was too much like her father.

There was a quick knock at the door, and then Drake peeked inside. "Are you okay?"

Dee Dee glared at him. "Please stay out of my room."

"You yelled my name. I thought something was wrong."

Dee Dee's gaze focused on Drake's chiseled arms and bare chest. She averted her eyes and picked up her cell phone to check the time. "It's four in the morning. Why are you still awake?"

He sat down at the foot of the bed, put his head in his hands, and rubbed his face. "I couldn't sleep. Just the thought of someone stalking you and Natua has me really shaken up." He straightened, then reached for Dee Dee's hand and squeezed it. "If you or Natua had been attacked, I don't know what I would have done."

Was Drake actually admitting that he didn't have all the answers?

"I know things haven't been that great between us lately," he continued, "but I hope you know how much I love you and need you in my life."

Dee Dee raised her free hand in protest. This was not a conversation she wanted to have at four in the morning, with Drake sitting on her bed wearing nothing but his pajama pants. "Look, Drake, maybe you should try to sleep. We can talk about this tomorrow."

Drake dropped her hand and quickly stood. He cleared his throat. "Sure, sure. We can talk tomorrow." He started for the door. "Get some sleep," he said, then stepped into the hallway and closed the door behind him.

Dee Dee fell back on the bed. She picked up the spare pillow, covered her face with it, and screamed. Why, why, why was that man so sexy? She had almost turned down the covers and invited him to spend the rest of the night with her. But she knew that by morning, she would be feeling just as inadequate as she always did around "Mr. Perfect." She couldn't—no, she wouldn't—put herself through a life filled with sexy Drake at night and sermonizing Drake in the morning. No, thank you. She turned over and went back to sleep.

~

"Oh my gosh, I'm going to be late." Dee Dee jumped out of bed and ran to Natua's room to get her ready for day care. Her feet froze to the floor when she saw Natua's Princess Tiana bed. Empty. Fear clenched her heart as she checked the window in Natua's room to make sure that it was locked. It was. Where was she? Had she gotten up in the middle of the night and gone to Drake's room? Or had a psycho stalker come into their home and taken her while Dee Dee had been lying in bed dreaming about Drake? Dee Dee was frantic as she headed out of the room, yelling, "Natua, Natua, where are you?"

"I'm right here."

Dee Dee was flooded with relief at the sound of the precious girl's voice. The door to the hall bathroom opened, and out stepped Natua, draped in her favorite princess towel. Drake followed her.

Dee Dee pulled the girl into her arms and hugged her so tightly that Natua protested, "Hey, that hurts."

"I'm sorry," Dee Dee said, releasing her.

"I figured you needed to sleep a little longer," Drake said, "so I thought I would get Natua dressed and take her to day care on my way to work."

Some days, Drake was so good to her, she just didn't know why she kept resisting him. Dee Dee combed her hands through her hair. "Thanks, Drake. I appreciate that. I have a brunch meeting today with the producer from that movie deal I'm trying to work out, and I really didn't want to be late."

Drake smiled at her, showing off his dimples. "You go get that lead part, and don't worry about us. I'll get Natua dressed, fed, and off to day care."

Dee Dee thanked him again, said good-bye to Natua, and then went to take a shower. When she'd agreed to adopt Natua, she hadn't thought there was much to parenting. She had to admit that she didn't know what she would do without Drake's help. In her book, the CNN Hero Award should be given to a single parent every year.

All things considered, Dee Dee was in a good mood by the time she jumped into her Mercedes and headed out for her brunch meeting. So much had happened since yesterday, it felt as if her meeting with her agent had occurred a week ago. But it was only yesterday that Nick informed her she would have to audition for the role she had been salivating over ever since Michael Mavs had mentioned it to her. Michael was the producer—the one putting up the money to back the film—so she didn't understand why he was letting some two-bit actor like Jarrod Lovett make decisions about this film that were absolutely none of his business.

But she was sure going to ask Michael to explain himself the moment she sat down with them for her "audition." The very thought of Dee Dee Morrison having to audition for a part that she could play in her sleep galled her to no end. She had half a mind to take that money her father had given her to put toward a charity foundation and start her own studio, instead. But, if she knew Joel Morrison like she thought she knew him, there would be some clause constricting her use of the money.

That galled her, too. Her father was rich beyond belief, and the old man had decided on a whim to simply write his children out of his will. He eased his conscience by telling himself that his sons and daughters had all made a success of their lives, so they didn't need his money and would be honored to help him give it all away.

It was complete bunk, and Joel Morrison knew it. His children had been strong-armed into agreeing, and that was why Dee Dee had simply decided to hold on to that money until her father passed away. By then, she would be able to find some loophole to get the money away from his accountants.

She knew it wasn't right to be plotting against her own father. He was a good man. But she simply didn't agree with his vision regarding the money that rightfully belonged to her and her siblings.

Her father was the reason she had decided to start doing R-rated films. If Joel Morrison wasn't going to give her the money she needed to maintain the lifestyle to which she had grown accustomed, then she would have to find another way. That meant she needed to earn bigger paychecks, and the only way to do that would be to grow a bigger box office audience.

Dee Dee felt that she had reached her highest earning potential with the PG crowd. So, bye-bye, sweet little Daddy's girl; hello, R-rated diva. If dear Daddy didn't like the thought of his daughter going nude in films, then he shouldn't have stripped her of her rightful inheritance.

Dee Dee was pumped as she drove down Interstate 10 headed toward Santa Monica. She was meeting Michael and that ole turncoat Jarrod for brunch at Ivy at the Shore. The tables at the Ivy were a tad too close together for everything Dee Dee needed to say to them, and that was probably why they'd decided on this location. They thought that she wouldn't get them told if others could overhear. But they were wrong. Dee Dee had starred in fifteen high-grossing films, costarred in five box office hits, and worked on a very successful sitcom for nine seasons. She wasn't about to let them forget any of that.

Her cell phone rang. Dee Dee normally didn't answer her phone when she was on the highway. People drove like maniacs and would rather mow you down than move over to another lane.

So, she let it ring, figuring that the caller would simply leave a voice mail. The phone went silent after four rings, but then it started up again. After three cycles of rings and silent pauses, Dee Dee decided that it might be too important to ignore.

She picked up the phone, hit the button to answer, and brought the phone to her ear. "This is Dee Dee. What's up?"

"Why did you let that man spend the night?" asked the ominous male voice on the other end of the phone.

"What? Who is this?"

"I thought you were mommy material, but if you could let another man spend the night in front of our little girl…well, maybe you don't deserve to have Natua."

"How did you get my number? Why are you bothering us?"

"Why wouldn't your husband have your number?"

Okay, Dee Dee might have been married more times than the average person, but she hadn't been married so many times that she could no longer recognize the voice of any of her previous husbands over the phone. "You are not my husband. I'm hanging up."

"Hang up if you want, but you'll never see Natua again."

Dee Dee had pressed the button to end the call before she'd heard the last of his sentence, and now she tried to redial, needing to talk to this lunatic and ask him why he was so fixated on Natua. His phone rang numerous times, but he didn't answer. Getting that frantic feeling that she'd experienced that morning at the sight of Natua's empty bed, Dee Dee pulled off the highway and called Drake.

When he answered, she screamed, "Drake, where's Natua?"

"Calm down, Dee. Natua is fine. I just dropped her off at day care."

"Go back and get her!"

"I'm on my way to work. What's got you so upset?"

"That man called me. He says that I won't see Natua again."

"What?" Drake sounded frantic. "What exactly did he say?"

"I don't know. I can't remember his exact words. I was hanging up on him when he said something like, 'You'll never see Natua again.' Please go get her."

"I'm on my way back to the day care now. I'll take her to the house."

"Okay. I'll see you there, when I'm done with my meeting."

There was hesitation on the other end, and then Drake said, "We'll see you when you get home."

When Dee Dee hung up, she looked at her watch. It was 10:45, and she was about ten minutes from the restaurant. If she got back on the highway now, she could make it to her meeting on time. She could help Michael Mavs to see the light, and then she would get the part that she wanted. But when she pulled her car back onto the street, she found herself bypassing the highway that would take her to Santa Monica and instead going the opposite direction, back to Los Angeles...back home.

All thoughts of her career went out of her mind. Natua was in danger, and Dee Dee would rather die than let anything happen to that little girl. She sped down the highway, doing something she hadn't done in a long time—praying. She asked God to protect Natua, to keep her safe, and to allow Drake to get to her before this madman who had been stalking them could grab her.

Drake's car was parked in the driveway when she finally made it home. She pulled in behind him, jumped out of her Mercedes, and ran in the house, screaming for Natua, just as she'd done earlier that morning. She felt as if she were playing a part in that old movie *Groundhog Day*, doing the same thing over and over again. *Please let this nightmare of a day end already,* she prayed.

Drake came into view at the top of the stairs. "We're up here."

She stared up the steps. "Natua's with you?"

"Yes, I've got her. I'm glad you're home. Now I don't have to pack your bag for you."

Confused, she followed him into Natua's room and saw him throwing clothes into her suitcase.

"Why are you packing? Where are we going?" Dee Dee asked, before picking up Natua and kissing her.

"We're going on an adventure, right, Daddy?" Natua said.

"That's right." Drake turned to Dee Dee. "I've booked us a flight to Atlanta. We're going to spend the weekend at your father's ranch."

Dee Dee put Natua down. Same ole Drake. When the chips were down, if he wasn't running to God in prayer, he was running to Joel Morrison so he could help him pray. Dee Dee threw her hands up."We don't need my father," she protested. "Why can't we just stay here and handle this ourselves?" She was still perturbed with her father and really didn't want to see him at this moment.

"I called the police, and they suggested that we leave town for a few days. They're going to monitor the house for us."

"So, they really think he's going to come back here?"

"Since he got in once, they think that it is a great possibility, especially since he seems to be agitated by my presence."

"Yeah, but if we leave, he won't have a reason to come in."

"He won't know that we're not here. I called Carlotta."

"The cleaning lady?"

"Yeah. I know today's her day off, but she's agreed to come over and help smuggle us out. She'll park her minivan in the garage and then drive us to the airport."

Her shoulders slumped. "I guess you've thought of everything." She turned toward her room.

"Dee Dee."

Drake's voice stopped her.

He stepped closer. "If you don't want to go to your father's, I can cancel those tickets and fly us somewhere else...anywhere you want to go."

She looked into his eyes, and for the first time in a long while, she saw the man she'd fallen in love with—a man who loved her so much that he'd turn heaven and earth upside down to do her bidding. She'd fallen for that man and had thought she could deal with his love for God. But, as time had passed, it had proven to be too much for her. "It's all right, Drake. I haven't seen my father in months, and he's not getting any younger. I'll go pack and be ready by the time Carlotta gets here."

Four

Dee Dee felt like an immigrant hiding out in Arizona as she, Natua, and Drake crouched down in the back of Carlotta's minivan as she smuggled them out of the garage. Drake asked her to take a different route to the airport and to watch for any cars that might seem to be following them. When she dropped them off, Carlotta insisted they hadn't been trailed, but Dee Dee wasn't satisfied with her assessment. She kept looking around as they walked through the airport and boarded the plane, imagining the worst of every man who glanced her way. She couldn't relax, not even when they were on the plane, thousands of feet in the air.

"Stop worrying," Drake ordered her. "You and Natua are with me, and you're safe."

Drake's Bible was in his lap. Dee Dee remembered sitting with him in the evenings while he read. Getting "the Word" in his system every day had been so all-important to him. She had done her best to distract him and take his mind off of that Bible, but nothing had worked, and finally she'd just stopped trying. "We're running from a stalker, and you're reading that Bible like it's a normal day."

"I personally think there are only two times when we should read the Bible—when we're in trouble, and when everything seems okay."

Dee Dee raised her eyebrows. "So, in other words, you think people should read the Bible all the time."

"Absolutely."

Natua yawned. "What are you reading, Daddy?" She snuggled up to him.

"I'm reading about the Great Commission."

"What's that?"

"After Jesus died and then rose from the grave, He met with His disciples and told them this....." Drake opened his Bible and began to read. "'*Go ye into all the world, and preach the gospel to every creature. He that believeth and is baptized shall be saved; but he that believeth not shall be damned*.'"

Drake smiled in the way he always did during "teachable moments." He turned to Natua. She was asleep.

Dee Dee tried to stifle her laughter. "I guess that Bible bores her, too."

"Laugh if you want, but it's because of this Scripture that I publish Christian books. I believe that the books I publish are a method of preaching the gospel. The next phase of my ministry will be to produce films that deliver the message of salvation."

"You're kidding, right?"

"Not at all. God has given me this ability, and I'm going to use it for His glory."

"Drake, don't go into the movie business. You don't know what you're doing. People want R-rated movies these days. They certainly aren't going to pay for some God movie."

"Tell that to Mel Gibson when he was directing *The Passion of the Christ*."

"And how'd that work out for him? The man's life is a mess."

"But no one can take the credit for that movie away from him."

Putting on her headphones, Dee Dee turned to the television, encased in the headrest in front of her seat, and began searching for a movie. Drake turned back to his Bible and the two sat in silence while Natua slept.

Joel's butler/assistant picked them up at the airport. Dee Dee found herself searching the Atlanta airport for would-be stalkers as she held Natua close to her side. It was not until she reached her father's home that she felt safe and able to relax. Dee Dee had always felt safe in her father's house. She hugged him like she hadn't done in a long time. "I'm so happy to see you, Daddy."

"I'm happy to see you, too. When Drake told me what was going on, I prayed that he could get you and Natua here safely."

"You knew I wouldn't let you down," Drake said, as he came up behind them.

They sat down in the family room and spent some time catching up. After about an hour of conversation, Dee Dee's father asked her if she had contacted his accountant about setting up the funds for her foundation yet.

Without hesitation, Dee Dee admitted, "I haven't contacted him yet, Daddy. To tell you the truth, I wasn't really feeling you when it came to giving all that money away. But after this guy started stalking us, I changed my mind."

"How so?" Joel asked.

"Well, for one thing, while we were on the airplane, I thought about how easy it was for us to just pick up and leave. But there are so many women who don't have the means to get out of bad situations. So, I think I want to start a foundation to help women and children, maybe build a few safe houses and provide funds for the women to rebuild their lives."

"I think that's an excellent idea," Drake said, beaming at her.

"I agree," her father said. "Every other day on the news, you hear about some woman being attacked or killed. Good for you, Dee Dee. This will be a legacy you can be proud of."

"Speaking of the news." Dee Dee pointed at the 64-inch flat screen. "What's that all about?"

CNN flashed a billboard that said, "Judgment Day, May 21, 2011." Then a reporter interviewed a few people who talked about a radio host by the name of Harold Camping, who'd told them that the world would come to an end on May 21 at six in the evening.

Joel turned the television off.

"Turn it back on, Daddy," Dee Dee pleaded frantically. "Didn't you hear them? They're talking about the end of the world."

"Honey, you can't worry about things like that," her father said. "The Bible tells us that no man knows the day or the hour when the world will end."

She turned the television back on and listened while the story continued. When the news reporter went on to another topic, Dee Dee turned back to her father. "Those people are spending all their money. They've stopped paying their bills."

Drake shook his head. "It's sad how people can be so deceived."

"Deceived? How are they being deceived?" Dee Dee demanded. "That man told them that the world, as we know it, will end on May twenty-first. You don't know for sure that the world won't end tomorrow."

Drake moved closer and put his arms around her. "I believe God's Word over the word of some man I've never met. And besides, this man also predicted that the world would end back in the nineties, and nothing happened then, either."

Dee Dee pushed Drake away. "Are you telling me that you knew about this?"

"Knew about what?"

"About this man claiming that the world would end this weekend?"

"I didn't see a need to mention it. It's not a big deal."

"Not a big deal? Not a big deal?" Dee Dee pushed past her father and Drake, rushed outside, and ran out back toward the horse stables.

When Dee Dee was younger, she would always come out to the stables when she needed to think about something or just wanted to be alone. There were five horses in the stable, one for each of the Morrison kids. There weren't enough horses to go around for all of them to visit at the same time, since each of them had a significant other—with the exception of Shawn, whose longtime girlfriend had finally gotten fed up with his cheating ways and left him, and now Isaiah, whose no-good wife was divorcing him.

Dee Dee saddled her horse and jumped on. It didn't matter that she was wearing a pair of $500 slacks that weren't made for horseback riding. She needed to get away and think. Pants were the last thing on her mind. After all, the rapture was at hand.

Her father's property encompassed miles and miles of greenery. Dee Dee had always thought of the place as beautiful and majestic. And the world was so full of tragedies—flooding, hurricanes, tornadoes, wildfires, and tsunamis had become all-too-frequent occurrences of late.

As she jostled along, riding her horse like a woman bent on escape, Dee Dee thought about her life—an existence centered on self-gratification. It was all about her. Whatever Dee Dee wanted, she got. She'd been married four times and hadn't found a way to be happy yet. Even the fame she'd earned through from her career hadn't been enough. She needed more.

Tears flowed down her face and drifted off into the wind as she realized that she had wasted her life wanting this or that, rather than being happy with what she had. She slowed the horse to a trot and then stopped it altogether. After dismounting, she tied the horse to a pine tree and then sat down on the grass next to it. She couldn't stop the current of tears that were long overdue, because she knew exactly why she was crying like a two-year-old who had been denied a favorite toy.

Her father had talked about the rapture countless times when she and her siblings were growing up. He'd exhorted them so many times about the necessity of accepting Christ into their lives so that they wouldn't be left behind. He'd told the story so often that even Dee Dee believed this thing called the rapture would, indeed, happen. But it had taken so long that she'd stopped thinking about it and simply gone about living her life. Now with this man saying that the end would come on Saturday, Dee Dee had to face the fact that she was not ready. And she doubted that she could get ready within a day's time.

Her father was ready. Her husband was ready. Natua was just a small child, and Drake had been teaching her about God; so, as far as Dee Dee was concerned, Natua was ready. *She* was the only one who'd be left behind. And the thought didn't sit well with her. Drake had brought her to her father's house so that she could feel safe, but right now, Dee Dee was more fearful than she had ever been. She would take a stalker over the rapture any day.

Years ago, Dee Dee had read the first book in the Left Behind series by Tim LaHaye and Jerry B. Jenkins. In that book, the rapture came at a time when everyone was just going about their lives, doing whatever they pleased, and then, all of a sudden, people just disappeared. What if she were sitting at the table eating dinner with her family tomorrow, and then their forks dropped on their plates as they disappeared and left her alone?

Did she want to be alone? Or did she want to go with her family? For so long, Dee Dee hadn't wanted anything to do with God or His rules of morality. She had lived a life of excess without apology. Was she now expected to grovel and beg the Almighty to forgive her?

Wiping her face, Dee Dee looked heavenward and said, "My father says that no man knows the day that You will return. If that's true, then this man who is claiming that judgment day will dawn tomorrow has to be wrong...right?"

She waited a moment, hoping that she might actually hear the voice of God for the first time in her life. However, she didn't hear anything but the wind softly blowing.

She tried again. "I don't want the rapture to come tomorrow. I'm not ready, and You know that I'm not."

That was it. That was all that Dee Dee had to say to God. She climbed back on her horse and trotted back to the house. She would spend her time with her family and then wait out the end of the world.

Five

Drake received a call from the Los Angeles Police Department at around ten that evening. Dee Dee had gone upstairs to put Natua to bed, and he'd expected her to return, but an hour had passed with no sign of her. So, he went to find his wife. She had been acting strangely ever since learning that a lunatic was predicting the world would end tomorrow. Since Dee Dee had grown up in a Bible-believing Christian home, Drake had assumed that she was familiar with what the Bible said—that no man would know the day or hour when Jesus would return—and that she wouldn't be fooled by someone claiming that he had pinpointed the day of judgment.

The rapture wasn't an event that believers could put on their schedule, just to make sure they repented of all their sins one day prior. God designed this thing to be a mystery to believers. Drake had no clue when the rapture was going to occur, nor could he fathom how so many people would simply disappear from the face of the earth at the same time. It wasn't his job to figure all of that out. All he was required to do was to have faith in God and be ready for the journey.

It saddened him that his wife wasn't ready. But at least he could bring her some good news about another matter being resolved.

He knocked on her bedroom door. "Dee Dee? Are you in there?"

"It's unlocked," she called back.

Drake opened the door and walked into her bedroom. His room was across the hall. The last time they'd stayed with her father, they'd shared the same bed, but Dee Dee had been trying to deceive her father back then. Joel now knew that they were separated, so there was no need to keep up the charade.

"I have good news," he said as he lowered himself into the chair next to her bed.

Dee Dee was sitting cross-legged on the bed with her laptop in front of her. She closed it and looked up at him.

"The police caught the guy who's been stalking you."

Her eyes lit up like a kid's on Christmas morning. "You're kidding. They got him that fast?"

"Apparently he just walked up to the door as if he lived there. When the police officer stopped him, the crazed man told him that he was your husband and said he was there to get Natua." A smirk creased his lips. "He also told the officer how unfaithful you are." Drake couldn't help it—he laughed out loud.

Dee Dee picked up a pillow and threw it at him. "It's not funny. This is crazy. How can this man think he's married to me?"

"I don't know." Drake gave a sly grin. "Do you have another husband out there that you didn't tell me about?"

"Ha ha. I have no need for a fifth husband, thank you very much."

"I know you don't, because number four is all you need." Drake looked into Dee Dee's eyes, daring her to disagree with him.

Dee Dee broke eye contact, looking down at her polished toenails. "I just don't get this, Drake. Why would this guy stalk me? And why in the world would he think he's married to me?"

"It is strange, but some people attach themselves to celebrities and lose all rational thought. I heard about a case with David Letterman where this woman thought she was married to him. She even accused him of sending her messages through the television screen. When it became clear to her that she really wasn't David Letterman's wife, the woman committed suicide."

"That's terrible," Dee Dee murmured. She frowned. "So, do you think I met this guy somewhere? Or did he see me in a movie and then begin fantasizing that he was married to me?"

Drake chuckled. "I can't say I blame him. I've fantasized about you for years now."

Again, she looked away.

"The detective wants us to fly back tomorrow, so you can get a look at this guy. They'd like to know if you've seen him somewhere."

Dee Dee's eyes widened with fear. "I can't leave here tomorrow."

"The police really want to get the ball rolling on this guy. They don't want him back on the street."

"I'm not leaving my father." Dee Dee got out of bed and paced the floor. "The world might end tomorrow, and you want me to go home, when I might never see my father again. I can't do it."

Drake stood up and went to his wife. He put his hands on her shoulders. "What can I do to convince you that the world isn't going to end tomorrow at six in the evening?"

"Be here at six-oh-one tomorrow evening."

She said those words with such longing that Drake found a reason to hope again. Was his wife ready to give him another chance? He looked into her eyes and saw something there that had been missing for months. "Don't tell me you'd miss me if I wasn't here."

She stepped out of his reach and turned her back on him.

He grasped her shoulder again and turned her around to face him. "Tell me, Dee, would you miss me or not?"

Tears filled her eyes. "I don't want to be alone," she admitted.

"But do you want to be with me?"

"I don't know how to answer that, Drake."

He lifted her chin with one finger as he lowered his head, and then he kissed her with all the hunger he'd felt ever since she'd imposed this miserable separation on him.

When their lips parted, Drake released her and stepped back. "It's a simple question, Dee. Either you want me or you don't." With that, he turned and exited the room, leaving her alone with her thoughts.

Drake went back downstairs to sit with his father-in-law and get as far away from his wife as possible. It was time for him to face facts. Dee didn't want him, and he needed to move on.

"What's got you so sour-faced?" Joel asked when Drake joined him in the family room.

Drake shook his head as he sat down across from Joel. "Nothing, sir. I was just thinking."

"Well, I hope you weren't thinking about giving up on that hardheaded daughter of mine. You two belong together."

Joel had always been in his corner. The man had introduced him to Dee, with high hopes that they'd hit it off. Drake wished he could give Joel a reason to hope that everything would turn out okay. But all signs said otherwise; no sense denying it. "She wants a divorce, Joel." With a long-suffering sigh, he added, "And I think I'm ready to give it to her."

Joel leaned forward and put his hand on Drake's knee. "I know she's not easy to deal with. But I've been praying for you two, and in my heart, I see you growing old together."

"Unless our friendly rapture predictor is right, as Dee Dee seems to think he is. In that case, I guess we only have until tomorrow," Drake said wryly.

"That's what I mean, Drake. Although you and I know that it is foolish to try to predict the day and time of the Lord's return, this may be just the thing that God will use to bring Dee Dee back to Him. I saw the look in her eyes this evening. She's scared. And I haven't known that girl to be afraid of anything." Joel leaned back in his seat. With a thoughtful look, he added, "I take that back. I think she's afraid of you, Drake."

"Me!" Drake couldn't believe this one. "All I've ever done is love her. What does she have to fear from me?"

"Since Dee Dee was a young child, I've tried to teach her about the perfect love that Christ brings. She ran from that love. But then she ran directly into you, and I believe your kind of love reminds her of the unconditional love of Christ. She just doesn't know how to accept it."

Dee Dee lay in the dark with her eyes wide open. She couldn't sleep, with thoughts of losing everything in just a matter of hours dancing around her head. She didn't want to be without her father or Natua. She didn't want to live in a world without Elaine or her brothers. To be honest, though, if the rapture happened tomorrow, Shawn and Eric would probably be left behind with her. Sadly, after all of the Bible studies and Sunday services their dad had made them sit through, only two out of five of his children were guaranteed a seat on the rapture train. The problem with that was that their father would go with them, not stay with Dee Dee.

She flung the covers off, jumped out of bed, and stepped into her slippers. Tiptoeing out of her room, she went to check on Natua. The child was sleeping soundly, as if all was right with the world. The girl was at peace and enjoying life. *And well she should,* Dee Dee thought, as she remembered the poverty-stricken environment from which she'd taken her. Natua had lost both of her parents to sickness and disease. She'd been living with her elderly grandmother in a home that was more like a hut than a house. The grandmother had expected Elaine to adopt Natua, but she didn't put up a fuss when Dee Dee had shown up instead. She had just wanted a better life for Natua, and whoever was willing to provide that life for her grandchild was all right with her.

Dee Dee was thirty-seven and had never planned on having any children. She had always worried that carrying a child would distort her figure in ways that she wouldn't be able to repair. She'd lost her second husband because of her selfish decision. Drake had wanted children also. But, just as she had told husbands number one, two, and three, "Ain't no baby coming out of this body."

She approached Natua's bed and gently touched her cheek. If she had only known that having a child would bring so much joy into her life, she would have put up with the extra pounds and given birth already. She just hoped that the self-proclaimed Bible scholar Harold Camping was wrong, because she'd really like to give Natua a sister or brother to play with.

"Sweet dreams, Baby Girl," she said as she patted the child on the head. "Sweet dreams for the rest of your life." She turned and crept out of the room.

In the hallway, instead of walking to her bedroom, Dee Dee found herself staring at the door across the hall—the door to Drake's room. Her husband. The man she had vowed to love until death did them part. At that moment, Dee Dee decided that if this was Drake's last night on earth, she wanted to spend it with him.

She knocked on his door. When she didn't get an answer, she knocked again and whispered, "Drake, it's me."

The bed creaked as he got up, and then the door opened a crack. He wiped sleep from his eyes and blinked, trying to focus. "Hey, Dee. Is something wrong?"

"No." She pushed his door open and walked past him.

"Then what do you want?"

She sat down on his bed and cast him a seductive look. "I want to have a baby."

Six

"Wake up, Sleepyhead."

With a yawn, Dee Dee turned over and smiled at her husband. She had spent the night with him, and now she wished for many, many more nights just like it. She wanted to stay in Drake's arms forever.

He held up his cell phone. "Your agent is on the line."

Sitting up, she took the phone from Drake and held it to her ear. "Nick, what's wrong? Why are you calling me on Drake's phone?"

"Because you haven't been answering yours. I've left you three messages since yesterday."

Dee Dee rubbed her eyes. "I must have forgotten to turn my ringer back on after we got off the plane. What's up?"

"What's up, she asks," Nick muttered. "Uh, you blew off the meeting with Michael Mavs, that's what's up."

Dee Dee put her hands over her mouth as realization hit her. When she took her hands away from her mouth she said, "Oh my gosh, I'm so sorry, Nick. I forgot all about it."

"I know you, Dee Dee. You were ticked off about having to audition for this part, and this was your way of telling them to shove it. But your little stunt hurts me, as well. Michael Mavs will probably never even consider another actor from my client list."

"Look, Nick, I didn't do this on purpose. I'm being stalked, and I was on my way to that meeting when the maniac threatened to take Natua."

"Are you serious? Why didn't you tell me? I could have gotten you some extra press coverage before your meeting with Michael Mavs."

"I don't want any press coverage on this. The police caught the guy last night, so we're safe for now. But I don't want anyone knowing about this."

"Are you flying home today? I can have the paparazzi meet you at the airport. We'll have photos of you and Natua in *The Star* by early next week."

"No!" she shouted. "I have to protect Natua. I don't want another maniac getting any ideas about abducting my baby."

"All right, all right, calm down. Just get back here today, so I can try to smooth things over with Michael Mavs. Maybe even get you another meeting set up for this evening."

This evening, most of my family could disappear. She looked over at Drake, and the longing in his eyes confirmed for her that she needed to stay right where she was—with her family. "I'm not coming home today, Nick. I'll call you when I get back in town." She hit the end button and handed Drake back his phone.

Drake frowned. "Nick wants you to do something today?"

Dee Dee put her arms around his neck. "He might. But I want to do some things with my family today. Starting with my husband, right now." Her eyebrows lifted in an invitation.

Drake didn't need much convincing. He lowered his head and kissed her, pulling her into his arms.

Later that morning, after they had showered and gotten dressed, Drake went downstairs to see about breakfast, while Dee Dee went to wake Natua, give her a bath, and dress her.

"What are we doing today?" Natua asked, as she and Dee Dee walked hand in hand down the stairs.

"Anything you want."

"I wanna ride the horses."

"All right, then. Let's eat breakfast, and then we'll go see about the horses."

Natua skipped to the kitchen, chanting in singsong, "Yeah, we're going to ride the horses."

The table was set with pancakes, bacon, sausage, eggs, grits, and biscuits. Drake and Joel were already seated.

"How'd you get all this food done so quickly?" Dee Dee asked Drake as she and Natua sat down.

"Mary was already cooking breakfast when I came down here, so I guess I'll just have to cook for you once we get home." He winked.

Dee Dee blushed as a grin spread across her face. But then, her mind's eye replayed that CNN story about judgment day, which was scheduled for today at six in the evening. The smile disappeared from her face as she silently prayed, *Please, Lord, let him be here to make me breakfast tomorrow and many, many days after that.*

"What's wrong?" Drake asked her.

Dee Dee shook her head. "Nothing, I was just thinking." She turned to her father. "Are you going to say grace, so we can eat this good food?"

The four of them joined hands, and Joel began to pray. "Lord, we thank You for this new day—a day we've never seen. I ask that You would open our eyes to the beauty around us and help us to see You as the love of our lives. Bless this food we are about to receive. May it be nourishment for our bodies. In Jesus' name we pray, amen."

"Amen!" Drake echoed. "Now let's eat."

As the platters and bowls of food were passed around the table., Dee Dee turned to her father again. "Natua wants to go horseback riding this morning. So, I'm going to ride with her for a while and then come back and hang out with you. Is that all right?"

Her father almost choked on the piece of bacon he was eating. "I would love to spend some time with you. What do you want to do?"

She was tempted to tease her father for being shocked by the notion that she wanted to spend time with him, but then she realized that his surprise was warranted. Because he was right. Until this weekend, she hadn't wanted to be bothered. She'd allowed his decision about what he wanted to do with his money to come between them. How sad that it had taken some judgment-day prediction for her to realize just how much she wanted to be a part of her father's life. She smiled at him. "I want to do whatever makes you happy." Putting her hand over his, she added, "I'm sorry I've been so difficult to deal with these last few months."

Her father lifted her hand to his lips and planted a soft kiss on it. "You're always a delight to me, Sweetheart."

"Thank you, Daddy."

"So," Drake broke in, "am I invited to this horseback riding adventure?"

"Oh, please, Mommy, please, let Daddy come with us," Natua said.

Dee Dee's head shot up. She exchanged a tearful glance with Drake. "Of course, Daddy can come with us." *And you can have anything else you want, as long as you keep calling me "Mommy."*

The day was all about family, and Dee Dee found that she actually enjoyed doing what others wanted to do, rather than making sure that her needs were met every waking second. Spending time with her father, Drake, and Natua opened her eyes to see just how much she had missed out on while she had been more concerned about her career than the people she loved. The four of them went horseback riding and then saw a movie at the theater. They grabbed some lunch and then came back to the house, where Natua napped while the grown-ups played board games.

Around a quarter to five, Dee Dee yawned. "I think I'm ready for a nap myself." She stood up. "Are you coming, Drake?"

He set down the deck of Sequence cards he had been shuffling and stood up. "I guess I'm ready for a nap, too."

"Okay, well, you two go on," Dee Dee's father said. "I'm going to head over to the toy store to pick up a few things that Natua told me she wanted." He started to stand.

Dee Dee stopped him. "No, Daddy, please don't go anywhere. I just want to spend a little time with Drake, but I'll be back down here in about an hour. Please don't leave. I need to see you before six o'clock."

He sat back down. "All right, Sweetheart, I won't go anywhere. I'll be right here when you come back."

"Thanks, Daddy."

She and Drake walked upstairs and entered her bedroom.

"Are you okay, Dee?" Drake asked.

She closed the bedroom door and started toward him. "I don't know how I'll feel later on today, but as long as I'm with you right now, I'm more than okay."

"Listen to me, Dee. The rapture isn't happening today. We will all be here tomorrow."

"You don't understand, Drake. Since I was a child, my father told all of us about the Lord's return. He'd tell us that if we weren't ready, we would be left behind." She walked over to the window and gazed out at all the greenery, then lifted her eyes to the sky for a moment. She turned back to her husband, "You're ready; my father's ready. But I am certainly not ready."

"But you can be ready, Dee. You don't have to torment yourself like this." He rushed to her side and grabbed hold of her hands. "All you have to do is accept Jesus Christ into your heart, Honey. I can walk you through it right now."

Lowering her head, she let go of his hands. "I'd feel like a hypocrite if I begged God for His forgiveness now." She plopped down on the bed.

Drake joined her. "I don't think it's hypocritical to ask the Lord to come into your life, so that you can be ready for the rapture. But, since you feel it is, I won't push you. Just promise me one thing."

"What?"

"After six o'clock, when we're all still here, promise me that you will give God a try." He pulled her close. "You know what I'm afraid of?"

She leaned back and looked at him. "You're not afraid of anything. You've got Jesus on your side. That's what you've always told me."

He nodded. "I do have the Lord on my side. But I'm still afraid."

"Okay, I'll bite. What are you afraid of?"

He planted a kiss on her forehead and then one on her neck.

She pulled away from him. "Tell me."

He looked her in the eyes. "I'm afraid that at six-oh-one, you won't want to be with me anymore, and we'll be right back where we started."

She put her hand on his cheek and kissed him. This was the man for her—always had been, always would be. She had just been too blind to see it. "Hold me, Drake. Hold me and never let me go."

Seven

Drake woke up and glanced at the clock. 6:20. He climbed out of bed and tiptoed to the door, not wanting to wake Dee Dee. She had been stressing over the rapture since yesterday, so he decided to let her rest a while longer. He went to Natua's room to check on her, but she wasn't in her bed. He then went downstairs and found the child in the family room with Joel watching *Dora the Explorer.*

When Drake entered the room, Joel looked up with a sheepish grin on his face. "Glad to see you. I was getting worried that you and Dee Dee had been raptured up and I'd been the one who was left behind."

"Oh, so now you've got jokes." Drake sat down with his father-in-law.

"I thought it was funny, but seriously, how is she doing?"

"She's still asleep. I thought it best to let her get some rest."

"You two seem to be getting along pretty well," Joel noted with a smile.

"Yeah, well, it's after six o'clock, so we'll see if it lasts once she realizes that we're still here."

"Where's your faith, Son?"

Drake knew that he shouldn't be so worried about his relationship with Dee Dee. He had faith. Didn't he trust that God's Word was true and that no man would be able to predict the time of His return? So, why was he so nervous about what his wife would do once she woke up and discovered that he was still here—still loving her and still needing her in his life? Would she reject his love? Or would she finally see that he was the man for her? Drake hated that he was feeling the need to guard his heart again, but he could feel himself building a wall that would keep Dee Dee out.

He didn't want to try explaining his feelings to his father-in-law, so he changed the subject. "Hey, did I tell you about the progress I'm making with my new production company?"

"I wish you would let me invest in this venture of yours," Joel protested.

Shaking his head, Drake told his father-in-law for what seemed like the hundredth time, "I will not be the cause of further friction between you and Dee Dee."

"How can there be any friction, Son? Your production company will be promoting the good news of Jesus Christ. I put my money behind projects like yours all the time. What's the difference?"

"The difference is that Dee Dee thinks you should back some of her films."

"I have backed her films in the past, but I cannot support what she wants to do now. I will not put my money behind it." He said those words forcefully, and then added, "The Lord has been good to me. It is because of His good graces that I am a wealthy man and that my children are blessed. So, I think it is only fitting that we give back. That's why I asked my children to set up those charities. Can you understand that?"

"Yes, I can. I think God is smiling down on you and your children for the many lives that will be blessed because of your generosity."

Joel smacked his knee as he sat up in his high-backed chair. "Then it's settled. You'll let me help you?"

"Not financially, but I could use your advice."

"All right, shoot. What do you want to know?"

For the next hour, Drake picked his father-in-law's brain about filming locations, set designs, how to find actors willing to do Christian projects, and so on. They were so enthralled in their discussion, and Natua was so engrossed in her cartoons, that they forgot all about Dee Dee sleeping the evening away.

Dee Dee's eyes flickered open with the knowledge that she was alone. She bolted upright in bed and scanned the room. She lifted the covers to see if Drake's clothes were lying next to her, without him in them. But his clothes weren't there, either. She picked up her cell phone and checked the time. It was 7:30. "I slept through it!" she screamed.

She jumped out of bed and ran to Natua's room. The child wasn't in her bed, either. Dee Dee covered her mouth with one hand and put the other over her heart as she backed out of the room. She went to check Drake's room, in case he and Natua were there. But it was empty, too.

"I'm too late. I've missed them. Oh, Lord, what have I done?" She chastised herself for being too stupid and stubborn to accept Christ into her life when she had the chance. She ran downstairs to her father's room. When she reached his door, she knocked. No answer.

She checked the knob. It was unlocked, so she opened the door and went inside. Her shoulders slumped and the tears flowed as she realized that she was, indeed, alone. She trudged down the hall toward the family room, thinking she would turn on the news and see what they had to say about the devastation that had just occurred in her life. As she got closer to the family room, she began hearing chatter. Had her father left the television on? No, she knew those voices—they belonged to Drake and her father. Relief flooded her heart. She then realized they were discussing Drake's plans for a Christian film production company.

She'd never given Drake's idea much thought before, but the sound of his voice was like such sweet music to her right now that she could do nothing more than stand there and listen. As Drake and Joel continued to throw ideas around, Dee Dee realized that the production company would be no different from what she was used to working with—except for the fact that Drake would be promoting the gospel. Her husband had real vision, and she admired that.

Wiping the tears from her face, Dee Dee tried to compose herself as best she could before joining them. As she stepped into the family room, Drake stopped talking. His eyes had been energetic and glowing as he discussed his business venture with her father, but when he turned to her, Dee Dee noticed that his eyes had lost a bit of light. She was confused by that, especially since they had been getting along this weekend, but she'd address that later. Right now, she wanted to give Drake and her father a tongue-lashing for allowing her to sleep so long.

"Why didn't you wake me?" she asked Drake.

"You were tired. I figured you needed your rest."

"But you knew I would be worried when I woke up and couldn't find you. I've been running around this house like a crazy woman, thinking I was all alone."

"We told you not to believe that man's prediction," her father reminded her.

Dee Dee turned to him. "But ever since I was a child, you taught me to believe in the rapture. I just don't understand how you and Drake weren't at least a little concerned."

Joel lifted his Bible from the coffee table and flipped through the pages. When he opened it, he held it up to Dee Dee. "Sit down next to your husband and read this passage aloud. Matthew twenty-four, verses thirty-six through forty-four."

Dee Dee took the Bible, sat down next to Drake, and began reading aloud.

"But of that day and hour knoweth no man, no, not the angels of heaven, but my Father only. But as the days of Noe were, so shall also the coming of the Son of man be. For as in the days that were before the flood they were eating and drinking, marrying and giving in marriage, until the day that Noe entered into the ark, and knew not until the flood came, and took them all away; so shall also the coming of the Son of man be. Then shall two be in the field; the one shall be taken, and the other left. Two women shall be grinding at the mill; the one shall be taken, and the other left. Watch therefore: for ye know not what hour your Lord doth come. But know this, that if the goodman of the house had known in what watch the thief would come, he would have watched, and would not have suffered his house to be broken up. Therefore be ye also ready: for in such an hour as ye think not the Son of man cometh."

Dee Dee closed the Bible and set it back down on the coffee table. She turned to Drake. "So, is this why you weren't worried?"

He nodded. "I tried to tell you that the Bible says no man knows the day of the Lord's return. But it also tells us to be ready, because He will come when we don't expect Him."

She lowered her head and put her hands in her lap. "When I woke up and thought that you all were gone, I worried that I'd missed my chance to be ready for God." She let out a bitter laugh as she lifted her eyes to her father. "The funny thing is, I never thought I wanted anything to do with God, but now I'm not so sure."

"Sweetheart, I'm thrilled to hear you say this." Her father smiled. "If it took a misguided man and his false prophecy to get you to see that you really do need God, then this was a worthy experience."

She grinned sheepishly. "Well, now that I know I have time, I'd like to think about this a little more."

Natua came over and sat on her lap. "Mommy, I want to watch *Dora*. Change the channel."

"*Dora*'s not on right now, honey. But don't worry. God willing, you'll have many more years to watch your favorite show," she said with renewed confidence.

Eight

During the plane ride home on Sunday, Dee Dee had much on her mind. She had left home running from a stalker, who had then become the least of her worries once she'd been confronted with her godless lifestyle and the possibility of losing her family to the rapture. The experience had gripped her heart with so much fear that she'd finally realized she didn't want to live without God anymore. But she didn't know what would happen to her career if became a Christian. What did God expect her to do with the rest of her life? She didn't have the answers, so she turned to Drake and began asking him questions about his production company.

Drake answered her questions freely, but after the fifth question, he said, "You've never been this interested in what I'm doing. What gives? Are you interested in starring in a film I'm producing?"

"I don't know about that, Drake. I doubt if I could grow my audience with inspirational films."

"You never know what God can do. You bet on me, and I'll bet on you."

She leaned back in her seat. "I don't know. I'd have to think about it."

When they got off the plane and headed for baggage claim, Drake drew Dee Dee's attention to a newsstand. "Dee, you'll want to see this."

She turned and noticed about three different gossip rags bearing her photo.

She held up her hands. "You know I don't like reading those things." She did her best to ignore the latest celebrity gossip.

He put the magazine in her face. "Read the headline on this one."

It said "Dee Dee's Stalker."

"Oh no." She grabbed the magazine and flipped the pages until she reached the article. Her eyes scanned it hurriedly, and then she looked up at Drake. "Nick did this."

"But you explicitly told him not to. Why wouldn't he listen to you?"

"He's trying to up my profile, make me seem dangerous enough to get that R-rated film I was going after." She handed the magazine back to Drake and stormed away with Natua.

Drake caught up with her, putting his hand on her shoulder to slow her down. "Look, I know you're upset, but I think we should pray before you call Nick."

Dee Dee stopped and faced him, grappling with her feelings about praying over this matter. If Drake had asked her to pray with him before they'd left town on Friday, she would have cussed him out. But now, as much as she hated admitting it, prayer seemed like the right thing to do. "Okay. Let's get our luggage and then go home and pray."

And they did just that. After prayer, Drake fed Natua some of her "perfect" noodles, and then he and Dee Dee together got the child ready for bed. Once Natua was down for the night, Drake grabbed the keys to his SUV. "I'll pick you up in the morning and go with you to the police station."

"You're leaving?" Dee Dee's heart plunged in disappointment.

"Yeah." Drake shrugged. "I know you like your space, so I thought it best that I go on home."

She inched toward him. "B-but...this *is* your home."

His cell phone rang. He looked at the screen, then glanced up at Dee Dee. "I'm sorry, but I have to get this."

He turned his back to her as he answered the call. "Hey, Bill, how are you this evening?"

Hearing the nervous edge to his voice, Dee Dee wondered who Bill was and why Drake would be nervous about speaking with him. And then she heard him say, "Dee Dee had nothing to do with the story in those tabloids...yes, it is true that she's planning to do an R-rated film...I fail to see what that has to do with our business arrangement."

She couldn't hear a thing being said on the other end, but she didn't need to. She knew exactly what was going on. Drake was speaking with an investor—an investor for a Christian project who didn't appreciate Drake's wife being associated with very unchristian projects.

Dee Dee felt bad for Drake. He had nothing to do with her choices in life, but he was nonetheless guilty by association. And the worst part of the whole matter was that she no longer wanted to have anything to do with that film. After she had prayed with Drake, God had revealed to her what she could do with her career. She hadn't said anything, because she was still trying to come to terms with it. But, at that very moment, the thing God had spoken into her heart seemed to fit. She had no more doubts.

In the middle of Drake's explanation, she took the phone away from him and held it to ear. "Hello, Bill? This is Dee Dee, Drake's wife. We thank you for your interest in his production, but he has a new investor. Have a nice day."

She hit the end button and then handed the phone back to Drake.

"Why did you do that? Bill is the biggest investor I have. Without him, my production budget is cut down to almost nothing." His nostrils were flaring, as they always did when he was trying to control his anger.

"You don't need him, because I am your new investor. Daddy wanted to invest in your project, anyway; I heard him tell you that himself. So, now we are going to use his money to promote the gospel."

The stunned expression on his face didn't go unnoticed.

Dee Dee laughed. "What's wrong, Drake? I mean, you did pray that God would open my eyes, didn't you?"

"Yeah, I just didn't know it would happen this soon." He looked at her skeptically. "What are you up to?"

"Well, there is a catch." She smiled sweetly at him. "God is moving my career in a different direction. I'd like to star in your film."

At that moment, he looked as if the touch of a feather could knock him over. "But what about the other movie you were interested in?"

She shook her head. "I don't want to do R-rated movies. I would be too ashamed to show them to our children."

Now Drake was stuttering. "Y-you said 'children.' So you do really want to have more kids…with me?"

"Duh."

Grinning, Drake picked her up and swung her around, then kissed her tenderly. "I love you, Dee. I promise to make you happy this time."

She looked into her husband's eyes and confessed, "You've always made me happy. Now it's my turn to make you happy. I love you, Drake."

About the Author

Vanessa Miller of Dayton, Ohio, is a best-selling author, playwright, and motivational speaker. Her stage productions include *Get You Some Business, Don't Turn Your Back on God,* and *Can't You Hear Them Crying.* Vanessa is currently in the process of writing stage productions from her novels in the Rain series.

Vanessa has been writing since she was a young child. When she wasn't writing poetry, short stories, stage plays, and novels, reading great books consumed her free time. However, it wasn't until she committed her life to the Lord in 1994 that she realized all gifts and anointing come from God. She then set out to write redemption stories that glorified God.

Heirs of Rebellion is book one in Morrison Family Secrets, Vanessa's second series to be published by Whitaker House. Her first series with the publishing house was Second Chance at Love, of which the first book, *Yesterday's Promise,* was number one on the Black Christian Book Club national bestsellers list in April 2010. It was followed by *A Love for Tomorrow* and *A Promise of Forever Love.* In addition, Vanessa has published two other series, Forsaken and Rain, as well as a stand-alone title, *Long Time Coming.* Her books have received positive reviews, won Best Christian Fiction Awards, and topped best-sellers lists, including *Essence.* Vanessa is the recipient of numerous awards, including the Best Christian

Fiction Mahogany Award 2003 and the Red Rose Award for Excellence in Christian Fiction 2004, and she was nominated for the NAACP Image Award (Christian Fiction) 2004.

Vanessa is a dedicated Christian and devoted mother. She graduated from Capital University in Columbus, Ohio, with a degree in organizational communication. In 2007, Vanessa was ordained by her church as an exhorter. Vanessa believes this was the right position for her because God has called her to exhort readers and to help them rediscover their places with the Lord.

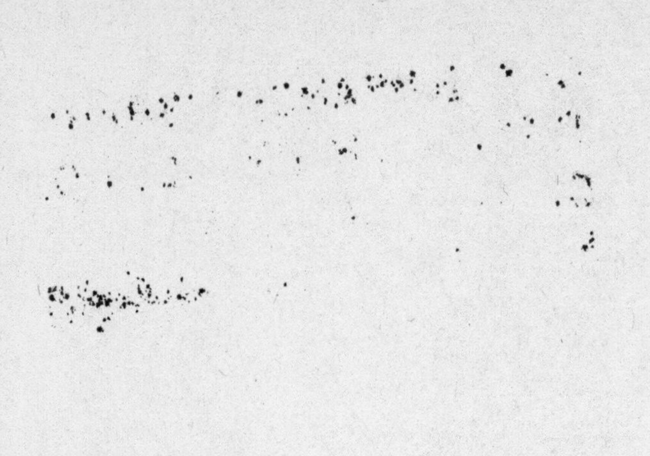